The
Interrogation Room

It was a place of lies. The police knew that from bitter experience. A gray cubicle with glass for one wall and a locked door for another, it was, for lack of better words, called an interrogation room. The young woman who sat across the beige Formica-topped table from Lieutenant David Sharp and Lieutenant Steven Riles looked as if she had already been interrogated by the father of all lies and copped a plea signed in warm blood. Yet both cops, even before they gently but thoroughly tore into her, wanted to believe Mary Dammon, largely because she looked so hurt and so cute. Pain and beauty in the same package—always a bestseller, even with cops as weary as Sharp and Riles.

Christopher Pike

Execution of Innocence

AN ARCHWAY PAPERBACK
Published by POCKET BOOKS
New York London Toronto Sydney Tokyo Singapore

AN ARCHWAY PAPERBACK *Original*

An Archway Paperback published by
POCKET BOOKS, a division of Simon & Schuster Inc.
1230 Avenue of the Americas, New York, NY 10020

Copyright © 1997 by Christopher Pike

ISBN: 0-671-55055-1

First Archway Paperback printing August 1997

10 9 8 7 6 5 4

AN ARCHWAY PAPERBACK and colophon are registered trademarks of Simon & Schuster Inc.

Cover art by Danilo Ducak

Printed in the U.S.A.

IL 9+

For
Scott and Shannon
of The Midnight Club

1

It was a place of lies. The police knew that from bitter experience. A gray cubicle with glass for one wall and a locked door for another, it was, for lack of better words, called an interrogation room. The young woman who sat across the beige Formica-topped table from Lieutenant David Sharp and Lieutenant Steven Riles looked as if she had already been interrogated by the father of all lies and copped a plea signed in warm blood. Yet both cops, even before they gently but thoroughly tore into her, wanted to believe Mary Dammon, largely because she looked so hurt and so cute. Pain and beauty in the same package—always a bestseller, even with cops as weary as Sharp and Riles.

Sharp was the young sexy one, Riles the doughnut eater pushing the fabled fat forty.

Sharp often smiled and flexed his deceptive dimples as he asked the good questions. Riles had gut instincts inside his beefy homegrown Oregon body. Both were what are called good cops. They respected the law, and more importantly they respected the half of the world who didn't carry guns. Yet they were both cynical: Riles with plenty of reason; Sharp, perhaps, from the company he kept. Of course there was the body of the eighteen-year-old kid down the hall, the one with the .38 hollow point slug in the right eye and the gray gook oozing out the back of his head. One look at him lying on a slab and staring up at St. Peter's pearly gates and most people would have gotten cynical really fast. Richard Spelling had been an all-American blond with good grades and a rich Daddy who was not only well connected, but also insisted on getting what he wanted. Yet this same impatient Daddy was presently waiting in the hall with his sole surviving child, a daughter, Hannah, and all Mr. Spelling's connections could not get the blood out of his son's eye.

Sharp and Riles had already exchanged bitter words with Spelling. The guy had yelled at them simply because he was the type of rich man whose soul had shrunk in direct proportion to the growth of his bank account. The two detectives had wanted to speak with Hannah and had insisted he not leave with her until they had. Sharp and Riles planned to tackle Hannah in another interrogation room, but first wanted to get to first base with Mary—legally speaking. But Hannah would have to speak to them because it was her brother who had been murdered. Both cops could still hear her cries in their ears after she had gone into hysterics when her father identified the body. She seemed to be calmer now, sipping a Coke and listening to her father's soft swearing.

Mary held the men's full interest now, though. She was not a truly beautiful girl, not by the standards of current magazine covers. There were slight imperfections to her features; her button nose seemed intimidated by her wide mouth and her dark brown eyes were large and deep but not perfectly matched. Yet the unusual combination still worked, and then some. She was the kind of girl that boys old and young alike wanted to hug. The overhead light was hard and white, not intended to bring out the best in any human being, but it could not dull the shine in her brown hair. Yet this same hair was dirty, and stained, too, dabbed with something wet—maybe blood, they couldn't be sure.

Before the cops even began to question her, they thought Mary might be hiding something. She looked down too often, and down

3

was the direction of the devil. If Mary did have something to do with Richard's bad right eye, then maybe she was contemplating how murderers burned in hell.

Lt. Sharp cleared his throat after finishing the introductions. Beside him Lt. Riles sipped a cup of acidic coffee and tapped on the black wire leading to the cassette player that turned mercilessly between them and Mary. The young woman had waived her right to remain silent, without their even reading her her rights. Mary was not under arrest, not yet, but her parents were on their way to the station, from some place out of town.

"Before we begin," Lt. Sharp said, "can we get you anything to drink?"

Mary shook her head. "No thank you."

"Are you tired?" Lt. Sharp asked. He had to ask. Mary's physical and mental state at the time of questioning could later be a major issue. Mary kept her answers short, her voice soft and weary.

"I'm all right," Mary said. She was dressed simply, jeans and a heavy red sweater. Her makeup was understated, just a bit around the eyes. Most of it washed away by tears.

"We understand you were good friends with the deceased, Richard Spelling?" Sharp asked. Richard's father had already told them as much. Mary shook her head.

"I knew Dick," she said. "But I wouldn't call him a good friend, no."

"Did you date?" Sharp asked.

Mary shrugged. "Once or twice."

Riles interrupted. "Was it once or twice?"

Mary considered. Her eyes took on a far away look as she did, but they were not unfocused. She was not in shock, she was thinking.

"We went out two or three times. But only once was a real date." She paused. "He was a nice guy."

"But he was not your boyfriend?" Sharp said.

"No."

"Do you have a boyfriend?"

"Yes."

"What is his name?"

"Charles Gallagher." A quiver of her lower lip. "Charlie."

"Where is Charlie right now?" Sharp asked.

A feeble shake of her head. "I don't know."

"You have no idea?" Sharp asked. Mr. Spelling made it clear that he believed this Charlie had killed his son. He was sure of it, in fact. Mary stared straight ahead.

"No."

"When was the last time you saw Charlie?" Sharp asked.

"Tonight."

Sharp glanced at his watch. It was three-fifteen Saturday morning.

"When?" he asked. "An hour ago? Six hours ago?"

"I said goodbye to him around nine." She shrugged. "We had pizza together at the Pizza Palace."

"Then where did he go?" Sharp asked.

"I don't know. I thought he went home."

They had already sent a car to Charlie's house. He was not there. Sharp told Mary as much and got no reaction. He leaned forward while Riles sipped his coffee.

"Did Charlie say he was going home?" Sharp asked.

"Yeah."

"Why? I mean, it was Friday night? Why was he going home so early? Why weren't the two of you staying out longer?"

A long pause. "He said he was tired."

"Can you say exactly what time he left the Pizza Palace?" Riles asked. Mary was wearing a watch.

"No. It was just around nine."

"Are you worried about Charlie?" Sharp asked.

Mary took a breath. "Yeah."

"What are you worried about?" Sharp asked.

She looked down. "You say he's missing. It's late. Shouldn't I be worried?"

"I suppose," Sharp said. "How well did Charlie know Dick?"

"He knew him. We all go to school together."

"Maple High?" Sharp asked.

"Yeah."

"You're all seniors?" Sharp knew Dick had not only been a senior, but president of the school. A young man with a future except for that damn bullet in his brain.

"Yeah," Mary said.

"What was Charlie and Dick's relationship?" Sharp asked.

"What do you mean?"

"You know. Were they close friends?"

"No."

"Did they like each other?"

Mary hesitated. "Not really."

"Did they hate each other?" Sharp asked.

Mary was firm. "No."

"Were they both interested in you romantically?" Riles interrupted.

Mary thought for a long time. "Dick liked me. But Charlie was definitely my boyfriend."

"What we're asking," Sharp said, "is if there was any jealousy between Dick and Charlie?" Mr. Spelling already said that was why Charlie had shot Dick, over Mary. But maybe Mary knew they had been talking behind her back. She studied Sharp before answering.

"You would have to ask them," she said.

"We can't ask Dick," Sharp said bluntly. "He's dead, and Charlie is missing. I ask you again—was there jealousy between them?"

"Maybe a little."

"Who was more jealous of who?"

Mary sighed. "I don't know."

"After Charlie left you at the Pizza Palace," Sharp said, "what did you do?"

"I ran into Hannah and Dick."

"At the Pizza Palace?" Sharp asked.

"Yeah."

"Did they see Charlie?"

"No."

"They came in after he left?"

"Yes."

"What did the three of you do then?"

"Drank Cokes. Ate more pizza."

"Did you leave the Pizza Palace with Dick and Hannah?"

"Yeah."

"What time?"

"Around ten."

"Did you leave with them in their car?" Sharp asked.

"No. Hannah came with me. Dick went off by himself."

"Did you see Dick again, later?"

"Yeah."

"How did that happen?"

"We ran into him."

"When and where?" Sharp asked.

"At the Crossroads. Around midnight."

"What did you do with Hannah between ten and midnight?"

A shrug. "Just drove around."

"For two hours?" Riles interrupted.

"It could have been an hour."

Sharp frowned. He was taping, he was not taking notes. But he needed neither with his excellent memory. "There is a big difference between two hours and an hour, Mary," he pointed out.

Mary smiled faintly, maybe sadly. "Not on a Friday night."

"Had any of you been drinking?"

"No."

"Drugs? Pot?"

"No."

"You're sure?"

Mary paused. "I was sober. But Dick might have been drinking beer, I'm not sure."

"When you met Dick at the Crossroads," Sharp said, "did you smell beer on him?"

"Maybe."

"This was at midnight?"

"Yeah."

"What was he doing there?"

"Just sitting in his car."

"By himself?"

9

"Yeah."

"Did you know he'd be there?"

"He'd talked about going out there."

"Why? Why did he go there?"

"I don't know. It was just a place to go."

"What did you guys do there?"

"Nothing."

"You must have done something?"

"We talked, walked around a bit. We didn't do much."

"How long were you there?"

"An hour or so."

"Did you all leave together?" Sharp asked.

"No. Hannah and I left together." She paused. "Dick was sitting in his car when we left."

"How was he?"

"All right."

"Was he upset?"

"No." Mary paused. "Why would he be upset?"

"Maybe he was upset over you."

"No."

"When you were there, did he talk about Charlie?"

"No. Maybe. I don't know."

"Was Charlie around?"

"No."

"So about midnight you left Dick sitting alone in his car at the Crossroads?"

"Yeah."

10

"Was he leaving? Did he say he was leaving?"

"We thought he was."

"Did you see his car lights follow you?"

"No."

"Was that the last you saw of him?"

"Yeah."

"Then what happened?"

"Hannah and I just drove around for a while. Then later we ran into Deputy Howard in town and he told us about Dick."

"What time was that?"

"Around two."

"So between one and two you just drove around?"

"Yeah."

"You two drove around a lot tonight. You and Hannah."

"I guess."

"Is she a good friend?" Sharp asked.

"We're friends."

"How did Hannah react when Deputy Howard said her brother was dead?"

"Howard didn't tell us anything. He just said we were to come down to the station." Mary paused. "But Hannah freaked when she heard her brother was dead."

"The two were close?"

"Yeah. They're the same age. They're twins."

"But not identical twins," Riles muttered.

Mary stared at him as if he were an idiot. "No. They're not identical—they can't be. One's a guy and the other's a girl."

It was Sharp's turn to sigh. "Mary, you know Dick is lying down the hall with a bullet in his head. Do you have any idea who might have killed him?"

"No."

"Could Charlie have killed him?"

She blinked. "No."

"Are you sure?"

"Yes."

"How can you be so sure? Dick is dead and Charlie is missing."

Mary swallowed. "Charlie is a nice guy. He couldn't kill anyone."

"That's not what Mr. Spelling says. He says Charlie definitely killed Dick."

Mary was bitter. "Mr. Spelling doesn't know Charlie. He doesn't know anything."

"He's the richest man in the county," Riles muttered.

Mary scowled at him. "Does that make him an authority on my boyfriend?"

Sharp spread his hands. "Charlie will not be found guilty until he is proven guilty. We are questioning you because we don't want to make snap judgments. But we need more facts, Mary. Does Charlie own a gun?"

"No."

"Does his father?"

"I don't know."

Sharp continued. "Charlie's dad drives trucks long-distance, doesn't he?"

"Yeah."

"He's out of town now. Do you know when he'll be back?"

"No."

"Do you have any idea at all where Charlie might be?"

"No."

Sharp paused and collected his thoughts. "Frankly, Mary, several of your answers disturb me. You have many holes in your timetable, too much time when you were just driving around doing nothing. Also, I sense that Dick was more important to you than you're letting on."

For once Mary looked him straight in the eye. "He was not that important to me, Lieutenant Sharp. I'm sad that he's dead. I'm sad for Hannah, but I'm more worried about Charlie."

"Do you think the same person who killed Dick could have gotten to Charlie?" Riles asked.

Mary grimaced. "I don't know."

"Can you think of any enemies Dick had?" Sharp asked.

"He was popular. Popular people always have enemies."

"Name some," Sharp said.

"I can't."

"Did Charlie have any enemies?"

"None that I know of."

"What does Charlie do? Besides go to school?"

"He works as a mechanic for Dryer's Tune Up on Main."

"And what do you do? Do you work?"

"Yeah. At the library."

"Are you going to college next year?"

"Yeah."

"Where?"

"Stanford, Palo Alto."

"That's big time. You must be pretty smart."

"I do all right."

"Is Charlie going to college?"

Mary lowered her head. "No, Charlie probably won't even graduate."

There was affection in her voice, but also sorrow. Maybe even a trace of despair. Sharp studied her cute, tired face and tried to imagine her shooting Dick in the face and was surprised to discover that it didn't seem totally impossible. He wanted to reach out and touch her dark brown hair, see what those wet stains were. Maybe his hand would have come back red. One thing was sure, he was going to check her out before she left the station.

"Would it be fair to say you and Charlie are

from different sides of the track?" Sharp asked.

Mary looked up and smiled faintly. "Yeah. That would be fair." Then her head dropped and she added in a wounded voice, "I really love him."

2

Maple High had a total student population of eight hundred and thirty, and because of that relatively small number, everyone pretty much knew everyone else. Mary had been acquainted with Charlie, from a distance, throughout her freshman, sophomore, and junior years. But it was only in early December of her senior year, when Charlie fixed and then broke her car, that she decided she wanted him.

She told him angrily that he broke it, but he said it was about to fall apart, and he was probably right. It was a Monday afternoon when she pulled her sputtering Honda Civic into Dryer's Tune Up just off the town square. The car had a quarter of a million miles on it and it ran faster in Reverse than Drive, but she was hoping it would hang on until she could move to Palo Alto and start college. Stanford was practically all she thought about these days, although she had applied to half a dozen other colleges as back-ups. But to be at Stanford was her dream because that was where her mother and father had gone to school and met. Now if Stanford would just accept her A-minus average and her nonexistent bank account.

Maple, where she lived, was not the sort of city that sent many kids to one of the best colleges in the land. Located in southern Oregon, not far from California's Mt. Shasta, the town was at an elevation of forty-five hundred feet and often suffered serious snow-bound winters. Because of the weather the total population never rose above ten thousand, and that included tourists and passing truck drivers. Yet the surrounding pines and hills always inspired Mary. She was anxious to break away from her small town but she knew she would miss it after she was gone.

As she parked that auspicious day and got out of her car, Charlie looked up from under the hood of a Ford Explorer so dirty it looked as if it had unsuccessfully dodged a mud slide. He was pretty dirty himself, with an oily face and jeans. If someone had told her right then she would soon be head over heels in love with this guy she would have wanted to know the person's IQ. He wiped his nose on the back of his arm as she walked over. He had a wrench in one hand and a hamburger in the other. Yeah, he liked Pennzoil on his meat and bun. She wrinkled her nose before she spoke to him.

"Charlie?" she said as if maybe she had the wrong one.

"Yeah?" He had pretty blue eyes but they weren't dancing with joy at the sight of her. His black hair was long and stringy and hung over his broad shoulders like strips of leather. He took a bite of his hamburger and chewed slowly, his handsome jaw moving with a casual rhythm unconnected to her haste.

Mary was about to be late for work, and Miss Soulte, her supervisor at the library, was always looking for an excuse to fire her. Mary thought the woman hated her because she thought Miss Mary was no longer a virgin, which was not true. Mary was as virgin as an unopened copy of *Cosmopolitan*. She had a rich imagination and poor prospects, although she did get asked out regularly enough, but by guys who had thrown spitballs at her in kindergarten. That was the trouble with growing up in a small town. The male population was largely made up of specimens she had seen develop from sperm and ovum. Not that she knew much about Charlie. He took another bite of his hamburger and waited for her to say something.

"I need a tune up," she said.

"Shouldn't you see a doctor?"

She blushed, although she didn't think he was being funny. She gestured to her car. "It's speeding up and slowing down all the time, even when I don't do anything. I don't know what's the matter with it."

He studied her car. "It's old," he said.

She frowned. "Should I go somewhere else?"

He shrugged. "If you're in a hurry."

She glanced at her watch. "I am in a hurry. I have to get to the library."

"I never heard of anyone who was in a hurry to get to the library."

She sighed and put her hands on her hips. "I work there."

He set his hamburger down and wiped his hands. He finally smiled—he had a nice smile. "I know where you work, Mary," he said.

He offered to drive her to work and said her car wouldn't be ready until tomorrow. She said that was OK, a friend at the library could give her a ride home and a ride to school the next day. She didn't talk to him about money. She had heard that he was good at what he did and never overcharged. Riding to the library with him, she noticed he hardly looked over at her.

But that evening when she got home she was surprised to see her car parked out front, and even more surprised to find Charlie inside the house sitting with her mother eating cookies and drinking milk. He had cleaned himself up but still didn't look like a milk drinker. As her mother excused herself, Mary sat at the kitchen table with him and noticed for the first time that Charlie had a powerful stare. He seemed more interested in her than he had that afternoon. She asked about the car and he shook his head.

"I tuned it up and changed the oil but it's still ready to fall apart," he said.

"It can't fall apart," she said. "I need it until next September."

"It's a car, not a person. You can't tell it what to do."

"I don't know about that. It's my car. I can tell it what I want. How much do I owe you?"

He bit into a cookie. "Ten bucks."

"No. Charge me what's fair."

"Fifty bucks."

She frowned. "That's a lot."

He waved his hand. "You don't owe me anything, Mary. Accept it as a favor."

She was afraid she'd have to repay his favor by going out with him. Not that that was such a horrible idea, at the moment. Still, she wanted to do what was right. She opened her purse.

"Can I give you thirty?" she asked. "It's all I have right now."

He looked at her. "You don't owe me anything, I promise."

It was amazing how easily he saw through her, she thought. His unkempt manner didn't mean he was stupid, she had to remind herself. She put her purse aside.

"Thanks," she said. "I really mean it. Have you been here long?"

"Ten minutes."

"You drove my car over?" she asked.

"I didn't walk it over."

"Do you need a ride home?"

"I can walk," he said.

"No. It's cold outside. I'll give you a ride. Where do you live?"

"By the train track, off Strater."

That was Maple City's worst section, its own personal ghetto. Mary winced at the thought of anyone living there, but then decided it was better than fighting sandstorms in a thatched house in Saharan Africa. Charlie continued to study her. Once again he seemed to read her mind.

"I don't need much," he said.

Mary stood and forced a smile. For some reason his remark had embarrassed her. "I should take you home now," she said. "I have to study for a few hours before I go to bed."

He also stood. "I haven't studied since third grade."

"I should have known you then. Third grade was the last time I took it easy."

She gave him a ride across town, to a makeshift house at the end of a forlorn block. There was no front lawn, only a dirt space big enough to park a pickup truck and collect the trash. She had just pulled in his driveway when her car engine made a terrible grinding sound and then died. She thought she smelled something burning. Looking over at him with fire in her eyes, she yelled, "What did you do to my car?"

He shrugged, unmoved. "I told you."

She tried to restart it, but failed. "But it was working fine before!"

"It was not fine before. It's an old car."

"At least it ran! Now I can't even start it!"

"You just threw a rod."

"A rod? What does that mean?"

"It means your engine is wrecked."

She pounded on the steering wheel. "My engine can't be wrecked! I need this car!"

"I doubt the car understands that."

She pointed a finger at his calm expression. "You are responsible for this! You will pay for this!"

"I changed the spark plugs, points, oil, and reset the carburator. I didn't touch the engine."

"Right. It's just a coincidence my engine exploded in your driveway."

"It is a coincidence." He opened the door. "My truck's here. I'll give you a ride home."

Frustrated, she got out, pulling her down jacket tight. Usually in December, Maple was below freezing at night. Yet there had been no snow this year, not yet. The overhead stars were hard points of light. She chased him as he strolled toward his truck.

"I can't leave my car here," she said.

"It sure ain't going anywhere tonight."

"You're impossible, you know that?"

He grinned at her as he opened his truck door.

"And you're a bitch, Mary, did you know that?"

She refused to open her side door. "I am not a bitch. No one calls me a bitch."

"Get in and shut up. Remember, you have to study tonight."

She opened the door of his creaky truck. She spoke with scorn.

"What are you doing tonight, drinking beer?" she asked.

Charlie just smiled and said nothing. God, how annoying he was.

In the morning her car was parked out in

front of her house with a huge red ribbon tied around it. When she started it, she was amazed how soft it purred, like a new car. Only later did she learn Charlie had stayed up the whole night to rebuild her entire engine. He had practically given her a new car. When she called him to thank him, to pay him, he just laughed and told her to forget it. But she knew she was going to have trouble forgetting him. She asked him out and he said he'd be honored.

That was the beginning; that was the end.

3

Lieutenant Sharp and Lieutenant Riles decided to have a mini-conference in the hallway. After telling Mary to relax, they left the interrogation room and huddled next to a water cooler that doled out water as lousy as the coffee they made out of it later. Riles looked worried, but Sharp thought they were making progress.

"She's not being straight with us," Riles complained.

"She's eighteen years old. We're cops. It's the middle of the night. I'd expect her to have her facts a little messed up."

"No. A guy she dated is dead. Her boyfriend is missing. She's not stupid, she knows how serious this is."

"I didn't say she was stupid," Sharp said. "Just confused."

"You don't believe that any more than I do," Riles said.

Sharp considered the something he couldn't quite find in Mary's eyes. "Maybe not," he admitted. "Do you want to take over the questioning?"

"No. You're doing a good job. But I would like a second opinion. Let's get Dick's sister in here. But let's talk to her together. I don't want to split up."

"We'll have to keep Mary waiting."

"Let her wait," Riles said.

Before going to fetch Hannah from the clutches of her unpleasant father, they stopped in to see Dr. Kohner and dead Dick. Normally the body would have been brought to the morgue for an autopsy but the place had burned down the previous month when Dr. Kohner had accidentally set some chemicals on fire with his lit pipe. Neither of the officers was happy to see that Dr. Kohner was smoking a pipe as he worked on sawing Dick's head open. Riles was older and had seen many autopsies but Sharp had to take a deep breath as Dr. Kohner literally opened up half of Dick's skull. The boy's gray brain sagged onto the makeshift autopsy table and thick blood trickled down a stainless steel gully that had been set up to capture the overflow. There was a portable X-ray machine in one corner. Before picking up the saw, the coroner had taken plenty of pictures. Dr. Kohner looked up and grinned when he saw Sharp pale.

Dr. Kohner was a mixture of German and Japanese. He often joked he was a product of Germany's alliance with Japan during World War II, and it was true he must have been born sometime before the war. He wore a thin mustache as white as a line of sugar and his hair was closely cropped to reveal amazingly youthful skin. He stood firmly erect, and although he was always friendly, he clearly preferred the company of the dead. There was an unverified rumor that he had been a surgeon before he was forced into pathology for refusing to close a patient from whom he had just removed an appendix. The joke was that the patient had been his own father. It was probably all a lie, but operating on his own father would not have intimidated Dr. Kohner. He had once remarked that his only regret in life was that he wouldn't be able to perform the autopsy on himself. Seemed he wanted to see what was really in there. He gestured to Sharp with his pipe.

"Lieutenant," he said, "you are too sensitive a man for this kind of work. You should have been a baker."

"Then you could have fed me pastries all day," Riles agreed, patting his gut.

Sharp tried not to stare at Dick's brain. Yet the gruesome sight held his eyes. To think that all the boy's thoughts had originated from that three pounds of jelly. To think that just a few hours earlier blood had pulsed through the organ and an entire universe had been alive. But these thoughts, these observations, were painful for Sharp who preferred to believe that even the dead were somehow immortal. That was the trouble with police work. It was too real.

"What have you discovered?" Sharp asked quietly.

Dr. Kohner puffed on his pipe and gestured to a metal basin not far from the body. A bloody slug, mangled from impact, lay in the center of the container. With a gloved hand Dr. Kohner pointed to a small scale beside the basin.

"I weighed the bullet," he said. "A .38, no question."

Riles stepped to the basin but did not pick up the bullet. "We're never going to match that thing with the gun that fired it."

"But Charlie's father owns a .357, which can take .38s," Sharp said. "That's quite a coincidence."

"Coincidence is not proof," Dr. Kohner said.

"Not unless you have the right jury," Riles

agreed. He gestured to Dick. "At what distance was he shot?"

"Judging from the powder burns," Dr. Kohner said, "not more than four feet. It could have even been less. But I doubt he pointed the gun at himself." He added, "It doesn't mean he knew the killer."

"Playing policeman, Doctor?" Sharp asked.

"He probably knew the killer," Riles muttered thoughtfully. "He might have even trusted him. Or her."

"Mary doesn't strike me as a killer," Sharp said quickly.

"But you don't trust her," Riles said.

"True," Sharp said.

"I would like to meet this young woman," Dr. Kohner said, his gloved hands dripping blood. Riles scowled at him a moment and then shook his head.

"You stick with your end, Doctor," Riles said. "When did Dick die?"

"He was found outside I understand?" Dr. Kohner asked, consulting his notes.

"Lying faceup in the snow," Sharp said.

"Within the last four hours," Dr. Kohner said.

"You're sure?" Riles asked.

Dr. Kohner snorted softly as he picked up Dick's brain. The whole bloody mess had somehow swum out of the bony cavity. It seemed to shudder in the coroner's hands, as if his touch caused it pain. Dr. Kohner smoked as he stared down at it and both cops thought the smoke was probably upsetting any chance of detecting minute chemical compounds in Richard Spelling's body. Not that there was any doubt about what had killed the boy.

"I'd have to ask the young man to be a hundred percent sure, lieutenant," Dr. Kohner said. "But my estimate is, I believe, fairly accurate."

They left Dr. Kohner and had another mini-conference.

"That guy gives me the creeps," Sharp complained.

"Have you met a coroner who doesn't?" Riles asked. "I mean, who would want to grow up and cut dead people open?"

"Who would want to grow up and be a cop? God, did you see how that brain wiggled when he held it?"

"The kid isn't still alive if that's what you're thinking." Riles paused. "We have to see if Hannah's story matches Mary's."

"I have a feeling it will."

"That's what I'm afraid of."

"There is consistency in truth as well as in lies," Sharp said.

Riles snorted. "I think you have a crush on her."

"That's ridiculous. She's too young for me. Besides, she might be a killer."

"She's protecting her boyfriend," Riles said flatly.

"We don't know that. We don't know anything." Sharp considered. "After we try to match up their stories, what do you want me to press Hannah about?"

"The relationships between all these characters. I can't believe Dick wasn't jealous of Charlie."

"That's because *you* have the crush on Mary."

Riles nodded. "She is a honey. But then, they all are until they shoot you in the head. Let's go get Hannah, and try not to piss off Mr. Spelling."

"That guy was born pissed off. I think the killer shot the wrong Spelling."

"The night is not over," Riles said.

They found Hannah alone with her empty Coke can. Mr. Spelling had gone to the bathroom. They tried to whisk her away before Daddy reappeared but were not fast enough. The guy seemed to come out of a wall. He was yelling at them before they could even reach for their guns. Not that they wanted to shoot him, but it was somehow a pleasant thought.

"And just what do you think you're doing?" he thundered.

Mr. Spelling was a stump hit by lightning.

Short and squat, he had the build of a weight-lifter gone soft and the ruddy complexion of too many after-dinner whiskeys. His head was massive; it seemed to grow out of his neck rather than sit on it. He was also intensely ugly, even though his offspring were fair and attractive. Sharp and Riles held their ground as he approached. Spelling was the big man in town but they were the big detectives and that was all that mattered at the moment. Yet they were not out to offend him. They both felt genuinely sorry for the guy—he wept real tears when he had viewed his son's body. Sharp spoke diplomatically.

"We told you earlier that we had to question your daughter," he said. "We know this is a difficult time for both of you, but memories fade fast. If we can talk to Hannah now, it would be best."

"No," Mr. Spelling said. "I've thought about it some more and she's not to talk to you without a lawyer present."

"Why not?" Sharp asked. "Your son has been murdered. Your daughter was one of the last people to see him alive. She may be able to help us find the murderer."

"Daddy," Hannah said, touching her father's arm. "I want to talk to them. Please?"

Mr. Spelling chewed on his pain and anger. "How long will you keep her?" he snapped.

"It shouldn't be long," Riles said.

Mr. Spelling considered. Then tears destroyed his impatience.

"Are you taking good care of my boy?" he asked, weeping.

Sharp spoke gently, trying not to think of Dick's wiggling brain in Dr. Kohner's gloved hands. "Yes. He is in good hands."

They led Hannah into a room across from where Mary sat waiting. But they did send in Deputy Howard to alert Mary that they would be a few minutes. They thought they were being optimistic, but in reality it took them only a few minutes to corroborate the main points in Mary's story, at least as far as the timetable was concerned. However, the match in stories did not soothe their suspicions. The match was too exact. Sharp and Riles looked at each other and thought the same thing. The girls had gotten their stories straight before they had come into the station. Yet why would Hannah lie to hide her brother's murderer?

Hannah was an interesting-looking girl, not as heart-warmingly cute as Mary but pretty enough to catch the eye. Like her brother, she had short fine blond hair and clear hazel eyes. Hannah seemed much more animated, and not just because her brother was a corpse. She had a narrow chin and a way of focusing that made her emotions easy to read on her face. It was as if her brain had a thought and immediately her expression conveyed it. Yet that may have been deceptive as well. They had not been talking long to Hannah when they realized she was one shrewd cookie.

Her clothes were beautiful and expensive. Her dark slacks could not have been purchased in Maple, and the light sweater beneath her brown leather coat was yellow silk. It almost matched the topazes in her sparkling earrings. Presents from Daddy during happier times. She wore more makeup than Mary but she applied it expertly. In fact, she must have touched it up after her initial attack of hysterics.

Hannah dabbed at her eyes as she repeated the same story Mary had told them. When she was through Sharp looked at Riles and the detective nodded. Go for the jugular.

"Do you think Charlie killed Dick?" Sharp asked.

"No."

"Could you elaborate on that statement?" Sharp said.

Hannah spread her hands. She had done her nails earlier. "Charlie couldn't hurt a fly," she said. "What makes you think Charlie did it?"

"He had access to the right kind of revolver,

and we understand that he was jealous of your brother."

"Did Mary tell you that?" Hannah asked.

"Yeah," Riles said, without hesitating. A white lie.

Hannah was surprised. "I don't think Charlie killed my brother, officers."

"Do you know where he could be?" Sharp asked.

"He's not at home?"

"No," Sharp said. "There's no one at his house."

"I don't know where he is," Hannah said.

"What about Dick?" Sharp asked. "Was he in love with Mary?"

"He liked Mary. He didn't love her."

"Had he slept with her?" Sharp asked.

"I don't think so. You would have to ask Mary."

"But is it possible they slept together?" Sharp asked.

Hannah shrugged. "Sex happens." She paused and a big tear popped from her right eye. She stared at the Kleenex they had given her and her hands shook. "Dick was a normal young man."

It seemed an odd phrase to apply to a dead brother.

"Tell us more about Charlie," Sharp said. "Was he normal?"

"Yes."

"Please. Give us more than one word," Riles said.

She sniffed. "What can I say? He wasn't an alien or anything. He loved Mary and Mary loved him. None of this has anything to do with Dick. Why do you keep asking about their relationship?"

"We're searching for motive, for clues," Sharp said. "Hannah, we know this must be very hard for you, but please bear with us and we'll get you home as soon as we can." He paused. "Was your brother the least bit upset when you two said goodbye to him at the Crossroads?"

"No." A strange light entered her eyes. "Are you suggesting he shot himself?"

"No. We know that wasn't possible," Sharp said quickly. "At least it seems highly unlikely. There was no gun in the snow near the body. No, we are quite sure Dick was murdered. Can you think of anyone, anyone at all, who was mad enough at him to do such a thing?"

"No."

"He was school president. He must have made a few enemies," Sharp said.

"No."

"Are you sure?" Sharp persisted.

Hannah hesitated. "Well, everybody has a few enemies."

"Charlie?" Sharp persisted.

Hannah momentarily closed her eyes and took a breath. "Look, they fought once. Everybody at school knows that. It's no big secret."

"What did they fight over?" Sharp asked.

Hannah sighed. "Mary."

4

Two days before Christmas, Santa Claus set it up so that they could have sex. It really was Santa Claus who made it all possible; Mary's parents had to attend a Christmas party where her father was playing St. Nick. As a result her house was completely empty for five blessed hours. Of course, if she had really wanted to get Charlie into bed, she could have gone to his house. But the cockroaches scurrying over the floor—they didn't like the snow outside—somehow ruined it for her.

Charlie was supposed to come over, eat dinner, get his Christmas present, and then attack her. She was supposed to put up moderate resistance and then excuse herself to put in a cervical cap she had recently obtained from a clinic in nearby Sutter. That was the plan and she thought it was a good one. They had been dating a month and she had had enough of just kissing him. Really, she had never wanted a guy before. When she was in Charlie's arms, she felt as if she were at the center of the universe. He was either a wizard or else she was in love. And he seemed to like her as well, although he had never said the three magical words. She was not totally sure he knew what they were. She was going to have to teach him, oh yes, when she was lying naked beside him.

It was a fantasy of hers.

But good old Charlie was just too good. After eating a half pound of steak and three baked potatoes, and then opening the box that held the sweater she had stayed up many nights knitting him, he just gave her a quick kiss and turned on a football game. Now Mary liked football. She often watched it with her father, who was a big Pac Ten fan. But at that moment she felt like cursing the man who had designed the football. For God's sakes, she had on a light sweater and no bra, a pair of silky sweats that a stiff breeze could have vaporized. She was even leaning on him, stroking his hair, but the jocks in black were going for it on third and long. For some reason she just lost it then.

She picked up an old shoe and threw it at the screen.

It exploded, which surprised them both.

"Wow," Charlie said. "I thought you liked football?"

Mary got up slowly and stared at the glass on the floor and the hole in her parents' brand-new RCA big screen. She had not thrown the shoe hard; then she noticed that a golf ball had rolled out of the toe.

"This is terrible," she gasped.

"I don't know, the Raiders were going to lose anyway."

She clenched her fists. "I am not talking about the stupid game!"

Charlie stared up at her with his innocent blue eyes.

"What's wrong?" he asked.

"I want you to kiss me."

"I was going to kiss you later."

"I want you to make love to me."

His eyes got real wide. "Really?"

She lowered her head. "Yeah. But I didn't want to have to beg."

He stood and leaned over and kissed her deeply. He slowly pulled off her sweater and kissed her again. Then he just stared at her, all of her, and she blushed.

"What?" she said.

"You're beautiful."

She took his hand, wanting to put it on her breast but was too shy.

"I'm not beautiful," she said. "I'm just cute. Like you."

He hugged her. "Mary, you are a goddess."

They stepped on some glass on the way to the bedroom. They both cut their feet, but not too bad. But later she was to think maybe it had been an omen, the blood on the sheets. She was not one of those girls who had a lot of guilt over sex. Still, at the back of her mind, she wondered if she would have to pay the price for her joy. He loved her deeply even though he never told her he loved her.

School was back in session for only a few hours after Christmas vacation when Richard Spelling crossed her path. She had dated him twice the previous year, and the second time he had tried hard to get in her pants, but she hadn't seen much of him since then. He had supposedly spent the summer in Malibu polishing his tan, and now that he was school president he acted as if he was too busy for the likes of her. Not that she missed his advances this year or last. Yet she held nothing against him, Dick could be charming when he wanted to be. Today looked like one of those days. He stood smiling his rich boy smile as she collected a few books from her locker. Third period was in two minutes. Neither of them had much time to talk, but she supposed a big shot like Dick could be late, as often as he wished.

"Looking good, Mary," he said.

"Great opening line, Dick," she replied.

He took a step closer and propped himself up against the lockers with a strong arm. Dick worked out, played basketball. He wasn't great at sports but he liked to look great playing them.

"Will it get me anywhere?" he asked.

"No."

He smiled. "I heard you're seeing Charlie Gallagher?"

She had spilled some juice on the bottom of her locker. She tried wiping it up with last week's homework. "You heard right," she said.

"Why?"

"For the sex."

"Is that true?" he asked.

She was still glowing from December 23. Dick must have noticed when she turned toward him for he suddenly took a step back, as if dazzled. She enjoyed his surprise.

"He's a great guy," she said. "Everything I always dreamed of."

Dick collected his thoughts. "I heard he flunked American history. Does he have a brain?"

"He is a very warm and caring person."

"I'm sure those qualities will get him far in this world."

She smiled mischievously. "He has other *wonderful* attributes as well."

"Get off it, you can't be sleeping with that moron."

She grabbed her books and slammed her locker shut.

"Shut up, Dick," she said in a hard voice. "And stop dreaming about what you can't have." She started to step past him as he blocked her way. "What?" she snapped.

"I want to help you," he said.

"I don't want your help," she said.

"Yeah, you do."

"Get out of my way or I'll scream."

He spread his arms. "I heard you applied to Stanford."

She stopped. "So?"

"So what do you think your chances of getting in are?"

"Pretty good."

"Liar. You have a three point seven five GPA and an eleven hundred combined SAT score."

"I see you've been doing your homework."

"The privileges of power," he said. "You're not going to get in."

She paused. "I'm taking the SAT over."

"You'll improve a hundred points, nothing more. You have to face reality, Mary. You won't get in."

She would have snapped at him except that what he was saying rang true. In her mind, she always blurred the scores of the people who did get accepted. She just went about her business, studied as much as she could, and hoped by good luck and God's grace she'd squeak by. Dick was not simply trying to psyche her out, she sensed.

"All right," she said. "Let's have a reality check. What can you do to help me get in?"

"My father knows several important alumni at Stanford."

Mary frowned. "I didn't know he went there."

"He didn't, he went to USC, but he spent a lot of time in Palo Alto and big business types travel in the same circles. He even knows Stanford's chancellor."

"You're kidding?"

Dick held up a hand. "I swear. When you're standing on the fringe, a well-placed word with the right people can make all the difference." He leaned closer. "I've already talked to my dad about you. He wants to meet you."

Mary eyed him suspiciously. "And then?"

"What do you mean? Then you get accepted."

"And what do I have to do in return for this extraordinary help?"

"Nothing." Dick shrugged. "You can ask me to the Sadie Hawkins dance."

"I'm going out with Charlie Gallagher. I can't go anywhere with you."

He turned away. "Suit yourself."

"Wait," she said quickly. He paused, and

she stepped up to him. "Why is it so important I go to Sadie Hawkins with you?"

"It's not so important. But I think it would be the least you'd want to do for me after I helped you with the rest of your life."

Mary scratched her head. "We could go to the dance."

"Don't look so excited."

"You know what I'm thinking."

"What?"

"What else you might want," she said.

He was annoyed. "I don't want anything. Didn't you have fun last time we went out?"

"Yeah. Until you tried to rape me."

"I didn't try to rape you. I tried to seduce you. There's a difference."

"And you should learn the difference."

He turned away. "Have a nice day, Mary."

"Wait!" She grabbed his arm. "I accept your offer. I'd like to meet your dad. I'd like to go to the dance with you. But on one condition. I don't want Charlie to know."

"He'll hear about it."

"No. You don't know Charlie. He hardly talks to anyone on campus. He has absolutely no interest in the social scene. If I don't tell him about the dance, he won't know."

He grinned. "I always knew you were a tramp at heart."

"I'm not going to sleep with you. That's not part of the deal."

Dick continued to smile. "When you sign a contract with the devil, you never know how many clauses there are to it."

Dick was a jerk, but she still thought he was joking.

Later that same day Mary ran into Hannah Spelling, Dick's twin. She and Hannah were friends but not especially close. They had hung out a few times, at the movies or stores, but had never developed any continuity to their relationship. Mary liked Hannah and wondered if it would be wiser going through her to get to Mr. Spelling. Hannah immediately crushed that possibility after Mary told her what Dick offered to do.

"My dad will see you if Dick asks," Hannah said as they stood together in the parking lot, ready to leave school in their respective vehicles. Naturally Hannah's car was a tad nicer and more expensive—a brand-new Lexus sports coupe, with leather interior and Nakamichi sound. Hannah added, "But if I ask him he'll pretend I'm not even in the room."

"Why is Dick so much closer to your father?" Mary asked.

"I think because I remind my father of my mother."

"Where is she again?" Mary knew Mrs. Spelling wasn't around, but couldn't remember why.

"She's dead."

Mary made a face. "Oh. I'm sorry. I didn't know."

"Then you don't have to be sorry." Hannah took a final drag on one of the many Marlboro cigarettes she smoked before crushing the butt under the heel of her black boot. She added, "My father had her killed."

"You're joking."

"Maybe." Hannah coughed and wiped aside her blond hair. "I was never sure what happened to Mom."

"When did she die? How?"

"Ten years ago in a car accident."

"Anyone can have a car accident," Mary said.

"Yeah. But her brakes gave out, and she was driving a brand-new car."

This was a topic they had never covered before.

"How do you feel about your dad now?" Mary asked cautiously.

Hannah shrugged. "You mean, do I trust him? I don't know if that's really an issue. I'm his daughter, he buys me what I want and we get along OK."

"Sounds sick."

"Reality is sick." Hannah paused. "When are you seeing my dad?"

"Dick said tomorrow was good. Can he really help get me into Stanford?"

"If he wants to. He really does know the chancellor." Mary tapped out another cigarette, lit it. "You just have to ask yourself what the price is going to be."

"Dick says he just wants to go to the dance with me."

"Dick wants whatever he can get." Hannah let go a bitter sigh. "He'll get it all."

"I can handle him," Mary said.

"I was talking about the family fortune. Daddy is grooming him to be his heir."

"What about you?"

Hannah blew smoke. "I'm a girl."

"You sound like you have a pretty screwed-up family."

"Yeah. We're a work of art." Hannah coughed. "Do you want to get loaded?"

"I'm not smoking pot these days. I can't think straight the day after."

"What do you have to think about?" Hannah asked.

"You know, getting into Stanford and then going on to become a brain surgeon."

"But you still drink alcohol?" Hannah asked.

Mary had to laugh. "If someone else legal is buying."

They ended up drinking Seagrams 7 and Sprite down by the Crossroads, which was a boring place unworthy of its mysterious name, or any name for that matter. It was just a spot out in the woods, five miles from town, where two nondescript roads crossed. Yet because it had a cool name, people congregated there to get loaded, or lustful, or loose. When Mary and Hannah had finished half the bottle of whiskey they were feeling about as loose as two oiled belly dancers. The only problem was there was no one to perform for.

At least Mary didn't think so.

It had snowed the night before. They were surrounded by virgin white. The forest was quiet, the trees stood silent watch. They sat on the hood of Hannah's Lexus and let their asses freeze.

"Have you done it with Charlie yet?" Hannah asked suddenly. A moment ago they had been talking about the origin of the universe, and how God had probably gone and gotten drunk on the eighth day of creation. They were laughing their heads off. But now Hannah asked her question seriously. She stared at Mary with her bloodshot hazel eyes and waited for Mary to answer.

"Yeah," Mary said and burped. "I had sexual intercourse with Charles Gallagher on four occasions two days before Christmas."

"Where?"

Mary mumbled. "My bed."

"How was it?"

Mary hit the bottle straight. "Oh God! It was better than sex!"

Hannah laughed for a moment. "Was it everything you dreamed it would be?"

"Yeah, I think so. I dreamed about it an awful lot, and had some pretty good dreams. But he was great. I love him."

"Really?"

"Yeah. I love him. I'm going to marry him."

"Really?"

Mary giggled. "Not! I can't marry him! I'm only eighteen and I have to go to four years of college and become important and make lots of money so my parents won't resent having given birth to me." She attacked the whiskey bottle again and missed her mouth. Boy, this was what stinking drunk meant. She worried she would still be smelling when she woke up the next day, never mind what day that was. It was getting kind of dark all of a sudden. Hannah continued to stare at her.

"Is Charlie the first one you ever did it with?" she asked.

"Yeah, I think so. If I don't include myself."

Hannah lit what seemed like her fiftieth cigarette. She blew smoke into the cold air and the smoke turned to fog and drifted away. Just like that, Mary thought. Wow.

"I've been with ten guys," Hannah said. "But I haven't found one that I like yet."

Mary was amazed. "Which ten?"

"Mark Stradler. Luke Carney. Peter Fraizer. Jerry Rodrigues. Peter Fletch. The others you don't know."

"Unbelievable. How was Luke?"

"Like the others."

"Ten male bodies in a row. Jesus. How were the others?"

Hannah tapped ash off her boot. "They were not what I wanted."

The whiskey bottle fell out of Mary's hand and leaked brown liquid on the snow. She made no effort to jump off the car to pick it up. Hannah was trying to tell her something important and she wanted to listen closely, to be a good friend. But she needed to speak her mind as well.

"It's because you weren't in love," Mary said. "When you're in love it's beautiful. When you're not it's just dirty filthy sex. Loveless sex has no true spiritual meaning deep inside your soul. But love makes everything totally cool. Love is God's special gift to horny teenage girls and boys. It makes them feel less guilty."

Hannah continued to smoke as if she needed a nicotine transfusion.

"Did you feel guilty about screwing Charlie?" she asked.

Mary tried to remember. "Nah. Just a little. When my parents came home from their

Christmas party, I couldn't stop giggling. Then I felt like I should feel guilty. But I was so happy I didn't really give a damn. Did you feel guilty after screwing half the town?"

Hannah smiled briefly. "It wasn't half the town. Only a quarter." She gestured to the snow-covered trees with the glowing tip of her cigarette, and Mary thought she saw something bothering Hannah in her eyes. Her friend's next question was not normal. "Do you ever feel like running naked through the snow?" she asked.

Mary didn't have to think about that one. "No."

Hannah pushed herself off the hood of the car and stood. "I feel like it."

"Not! You'll catch cold."

Hannah began to unbutton her coat. "My blood is on fire. I won't get cold."

Mary just sat and watched her undress. "You must be drunk," she said finally.

Hannah stepped out of her underwear and modeled for Mary.

"Do you think I'm sexy?" she asked as if she were Rod Stewart or maybe his latest wife. Mary couldn't help noticing that the answer to the question was a definite *yes*. Hannah had an awesome body, bouncy tits out to the trees and an ass as smooth and white as Frosty the Snowman's illegitimate mistress. Amazing, Mary thought, but why was she being asked to look at a naked girl when she *was* a girl and really liked looking at naked boys? Charlie, in particular, lying in her bed half asleep. Nothing Hannah was doing made sense, especially when Hannah bolted into the trees and began to kick up snow with her bare feet and legs. Mary slid off the hood and struggled with the recent earth changes as she called out to Hannah.

"Hey, Hannah!" she said. "You can't do that! You'll freeze!"

Hannah didn't answer, but continued to run wild through the forest, circling the Crossroads, leaving tracks in the snow. Deer tracks, Mary thought in a moment of clarity. A hunted deer. Hannah didn't stop for a good twenty minutes. When she finally plopped down on her back in a nearby snowdrift, Mary feared she was dead. By the time Mary was able to drag Hannah back into her car and get the heat cranked up all the way, Hannah was practically dead. A frozen corpse. A casualty of the times.

The next day at school they didn't even speak of it.

5

At the police station things were heating up. After talking to Hannah, Sharp and Riles got flagged back into the autopsy room by Dr. Kohner. The coroner spoke to them while standing beside the body. He seemed afraid to move too far from it in case it stood up and walked away. Dick's brain sat in a stainless steel basin like a lump of gory pain and continued to bother Sharp, as did the stench of blood and death. Dr. Kohner looked as excited as he ever got, which was not saying much.

"I just received preliminary blood work on the late Richard Spelling," he said. "The alcohol content of his blood was point-two-eight."

"He was drunk," Sharp said.

"He was completely smashed," Riles said.

"That's good, we can use that, I think. Anything else?"

"Yes." Dr. Kohner lifted Dick's right arm to point out two scratch marks stretching from the wrist to the elbow. They weren't deep but they definitely were not self inflicted. "I missed these at first, I don't know how."

"I think you were just anxious to saw open his head," Sharp said.

Dr. Kohner smiled thinly. "Probably correct. Every good examination should start with the brain. But that aside, let me offer you my professional opinion on these scratches." He paused for effect. "They were made by a female in the midst of a struggle with the deceased."

"How do you know? Nail polish?" Riles asked, bending closer. "I don't see any."

"There was a trace amount," Kohner said. "I've scraped it free and saved it for later identification. Also the marks—their narrowness—would indicate female nails."

"Hannah has on nail polish," Riles mused.

"Hannah did not kill her brother," Sharp said. "Charlie is our suspect."

"For all we know Charlie is dead," Riles said. He nodded to the coroner. "Thank you, Dr. Kohner. Keep us up to date."

"I will keep you up to the minute," Dr. Kohner said, turning back to the body.

In the hallway, their favorite place to talk, the detectives huddled.

"We should see if Mary or Hannah's nails are broken," Sharp said.

"I already looked," Riles said. "Both girls' nails are intact. What we should look for is skin under their nails."

"We'd have to arrest them to do that," Sharp said. "Mr. Spelling wouldn't give us permission to examine his daughter. Are we ready to take that step?"

"No. We need more facts. Besides, which one of them would we arrest? Charlie's still our main suspect, even with the nail polish."

"Do you really think he's dead?" Sharp asked.

"It's a possibility," Riles paused. "Let's get back to Mary. We ought to be able to shake her up a bit with this new finding. Also, remember to play Hannah's testimony against her own."

"Mary might be too smart for that," Sharp said.

"That remains to be seen," Riles said.

But they were stopped in the hall before they got to Mary. A deputy brought them a witness. Her name was Linda Hoppe and she acted as if she were bursting to talk to them. On the short side, with her thin dark hair tied up with a steel pin that could have been classified as a dangerous weapon if it were any bigger, she looked like she knew something that could harm Mary or Hannah. Sharp and Riles were quick to usher her into a little office to talk to her. They turned on the tape recorder after Linda said it was OK.

"Are you two like detectives?" she asked.

"Yes," Sharp replied. "We're both lieutenants."

"Oh, that's so cool. I bet you carry guns and everything?"

Sharp nodded. "And we keep them loaded. How did you hear about Richard Spelling's death?"

Linda waved her hand. "It's all over town."

"It's the middle of the night," Riles protested.

"It doesn't matter. Dick was a big dick—but, I mean, he was school president. And to just get wasted like that, it's so cool. I mean, it's so dramatic. Like the guy is only eighteen or whatever and he has a bullet in his brain."

Sharp and Riles looked at each other and tried not to groan.

"You told the deputy you had something important to tell us," Sharp said. "What is it?"

Linda grinned with excitement. "I know who killed Dick."

"Who?" Sharp asked.

"Mary Dammon."

Riles coughed. "Why do you think it was Mary?"

"Because I was sitting right behind Mary and Hannah in Day Glow Donut two nights ago when Mary told Hannah she was going to kill Charlie."

Sharp tried to keep a straight face. "But it's Dick who's dead."

"I know that! But if she was going to kill Charlie then she was probably the one who killed Dick." Linda paused and looked a tad worried. "Don't you think?"

Riles sighed. "Can you give us the context of Mary's remark to Hannah?"

"You mean, like what else did she say besides wanting to kill Charlie?"

"Exactly," Sharp said.

Linda frowned. "I don't know. That was a few days ago. I just know she was real mad at Charlie and she said she felt like killing him."

"So she didn't exactly say she was going to kill him?" Sharp said.

"What's the difference? She wanted to kill him or she was going to kill him. I mean, everyone in town knows Charlie's dead, too."

"It's three in the morning," Riles muttered. "Why isn't everyone in town in bed?"

Linda beamed. "Because this is so exciting! It's better than 'Court TV.' Maple has a real live celebrity now!"

"Who?" Sharp wanted to know.

"Mary Dammon, of course. I know she wanted to go to Stanford and be somebody, but this way she's loads more famous, and right away." Linda paused and leaned forward. "Will I get to go to court and testify against her? Do you think there'll be national TV coverage?"

"I think we're getting a little ahead of ourselves," Sharp said. "Why was Mary upset at Charlie?"

Linda sat back and stared at her fingernails. "Because he was pissed at her for going out with Dick behind his back."

"When did Dick go out with Mary?" Sharp asked.

"Last week. They went to the Sadie Hawkins dance together. Didn't she tell you?"

"No," Sharp said.

Linda slapped the table. "See! I told you she was lying. She must have killed them both. Do you think she'll get the death penalty? She's eighteen, you know. They should gas her brains out. Dick was a great guy."

"But you just said he was a dick," Riles said.

"He was a total dick. But he had a great body. I mean, he didn't deserve to die." Linda paused and her eyes sparkled. "Have you seen his body? Is it all gross?"

"Linda," Sharp said with forced patience, "do you have any idea where Charlie is now?"

Linda considered. "Lying facedown in a pile of snow deep in the woods?"

"We're asking you," Sharp said. "Not testing you."

"But I told you, I think Charlie's dead. Why don't you ask Mary where she dumped the body."

"Because Mary doesn't think Charlie's dead," Sharp said.

"Well, she's lying, you know. Just because she's pretty and everything doesn't mean you should believe what she says."

"Do you believe Hannah was in on these 'double' murders?" Riles asked quietly. Linda firmly shook her head.

"No. Hannah loved her brother. I mean, she was his twin. Twins are supposed to love each other. I read that in my psychology class."

"When you were in the doughnut shop," Sharp asked, "did Hannah say anything to indicate she was mad at either her brother or Charlie?"

"No. Mary was doing all the talking. She said she was going to kill them both."

"But you just said she said she was going to kill Charlie," Sharp said.

"I told you *I think* she killed them both. Wasted the bastards."

"Now they're bastards," Riles said.

Linda brushed away the contradictions. "All boys are bastards, at least when they're in high school. All they think about is sex." She paused. "I know for a fact that Dick had sex with Mary the night of the dance."

"How do you know?" Sharp asked.

"I saw them doing it out in the school parking lot. In the dark and the cold."

"You saw Mary and Dick engaged in sexual intercourse?" Sharp asked.

Linda thought for a moment. "Well, I saw them kissing like they were about to do it. Other kids saw them, too. You can ask them if you don't believe me."

"Why shouldn't we believe you, Linda?" Sharp asked.

She was annoyed. "Because you keep asking me questions like you think I'm making all this up. I'm not you know. I didn't have to come here. It's not like I'm hoping to be on TV tonight or anything."

"Let's try to get back on track," Sharp said. "You say Charlie was upset with Mary because she went to the school dance with Dick. Is that correct?"

"I told you, Charlie was pissed. He wanted to kill Mary."

"Did he?" Riles mumbled to himself. But Linda jumped.

"Is she dead, too? Did she commit suicide? Wow, Mary is so dramatic."

"Mary is alive and well," Sharp said dryly. "Hannah is with us as well. Now let's clear up this point. Why was Mary at the dance with Dick instead of with Charlie, her boyfriend?"

"Because she wanted to do it with Dick?" Linda asked.

"We're asking you," Sharp said.

"Why don't you ask Dick? No, he's dead, you can't ask him. Why don't you ask Mary?"

"We will," Sharp said. "We'll talk to her in a minute. But before we say goodbye to you we have to ask what your relationship is—and was—to all these people."

"To Dick, too?" Linda asked.

"Yes," Sharp said.

Linda played with her fingers. "They're all my friends. I'd do anything for any of them. I mean that sincerely."

"But you think Mary should be gassed if she killed Dick?" Riles asked.

"Absolutely. Mary's nice and stuff, but she's also spoiled. She thinks she's so pretty and smart. Why, she couldn't even get into Stanford without doing it with Dick. Everyone knows that, you can ask."

"What does Dick have to do with Mary getting into Stanford?" Sharp asked.

Linda spoke with exaggerated patience. "Dick's dad can get anyone into Stanford. That's why Mary went out with Dick."

"But you just said you didn't know why they went out," Sharp said.

Linda was indignant. "I did not."

Sharp gestured to the recorder. "We have it on tape, Linda."

She sulked. "That's not fair. You use my own words against me. I have the right to remain silent. You cops have violated my constitutional rights. You're worse than the LAPD."

Sharp and Riles decided it was time to end the interview. They escorted Linda to the door and made her swear that she would not leave town before sunrise. They got stopped once more before they made it back to Mary. Deputy Howard was on the line. He had exciting news. He found the murder weapon, he believed, in the snow in the woods out by the Crossroads. It was a .357, he said. Sharp was pleased with the news but Riles looked worried. Sharp wanted to know why and Riles gestured in the direction of Mary's interrogation room.

"Do you really want to go home tonight knowing that that girl murdered two young men?" he asked.

Sharp shook his head. "Why two? Are you listening to that Linda? She was a clown. Charlie's still our main suspect."

Riles sighed. "I'm beginning to believe he could be dead."

"There you go again. I don't get you. Charlie's dead just because his dad's gun may or may not have been found? We don't even know it was his gun."

Riles spoke as if from experience. "A guy is a lot less likely to throw away a gun than a girl. That may sound sexist, and it probably is, but it's true. Charlie wouldn't have just tossed the gun in the woods not far from the body. If it is his gun."

"He might have panicked."

"After he killed Dick?"

"Yes," Sharp said. "He must have known that to be caught with the gun would be overwhelmingly incriminating. I say he shot Dick and threw the gun and ran."

Riles gestured in the direction of Mary. "We'll see. I want to talk to her before we all go out to the spot."

"You want Hannah and Mary to come with us?"

"Yes," Riles said.

"But why?"

Riles spoke firmly. "I want to see their faces when we get there. When we show them the spot the gun was found. I want to see what they saw—earlier. If they were there."

"How will we get them out past Spelling?" Sharp wanted to know.

"The back way," Riles answered and winked.

They returned to Mary, to the interrogation room. She jumped up as they entered and studied their faces. There was no mistaking the scrutiny.

"You were gone a long time," she said.

"A lot has happened since we talked," Riles said. "We think we may have found the murder weapon. We're going out to where it was found right now. We'd like you and Hannah to come with us."

"To the Crossroads?" Mary asked.

Riles glanced at Sharp and nodded.

"How did you know the gun was at the Crossroads?" Sharp asked.

Mary paused. Then she shrugged. "That's where you found the body. I assumed the gun would be there as well." She hesitated. "Do I have to come?"

"You're under no legal obligation," Sharp said. "But we think it would be a good idea."

He didn't say it, but he almost added, "*Now.*"

Now that Mary admitted she knew where the gun had been left.

6

The Spelling house was not only large but
was beautifully designed as well. Set in the
woods on a ridge that offered a view all the
way to Mt. Shasta in California, the house
was constructed with exposed beams of ce-
dar wood. There were four levels, each
sparsely furnished. Mr. Spelling had opted
for an open feeling. But each piece of furni-
ture was tasteful and expensive. While waiting to see the important man. Mary sat on a
ten thousand-dollar couch beside a table
holding an antique Chinese vase. Curiously
enough, neither Dick nor Hannah was at
home. Mary tried reading a magazine while
waiting for Mr. Spelling, but found herself
stuck on the first paragraph. She was more
than nervous because she realized, as Dick

had said, that the rest of her life could depend on this meeting.

Finally Mr. Spelling called her into his office. One wall was entirely glass, and framed a view out into the trees. The others were decorated with award plaques she couldn't easily read. Mr. Spelling sat behind a desk as massive as himself. Neither of his children took after him, physically at least. He was a bull of a man, with a swollen red neck and intense blue eyes that looked as if they could melt wax if he got mad enough. She had heard about his temper, yet at the moment he seemed relaxed, even in a good mood. She had met him once before, last year when she had gone out with Dick. He acted as if he remembered her well. After a few minutes of small talk, he turned the conversation to Stanford and Mary. Mr. Spelling sounded a grim note.

"You know that Stanford is rated number one in the country now," he said. "Their admission standards have gone through the roof. I'm not even sure Dick will get in."

"Sure he will. He practically has straight A's. I don't know what his SAT scores were, but I'm sure they were high." She refrained from adding *higher than mine.* She continued, "He's also school president. You know how colleges like stuff like that."

Mr. Spelling played with a gold paperweight

on his desk. It was a solid lump, three pounds of crude metal, worth God only knew how much. He appeared thoughtful.

"Dick has really tried to excel," he mused.

"Hannah doesn't do too bad herself," Mary said.

It was the wrong thing to say. Mr. Spelling made a face and waved his hand. He stood up and moved to the window, staring out.

"Hannah is hopeless," he muttered finally.

She felt bold. She thought he would respect that.

"You have high standards, Mr. Spelling," she said. "Hannah is envied at school. I consider her a good friend."

He snorted to the trees. "I heard you two got drunk yesterday."

Mary frowned. "Did Hannah tell you that?"

"No. But I hear what goes on in this town."

Mary forced a smile. "In that case we drank a whole bottle of whiskey together." She touched her head. "I still feel slightly hung over."

Mr. Spelling turned back to her. He smiled briefly but it was more of a reflex. "Personally I don't care if she gets drunk once a week. It's more her attitude that disturbs me. She has no sense of responsibility."

"She's only eighteen. What sense of responsibility does any eighteen-year-old have?"

"Dick is very responsible. I tell him to do

something, and it's as good as done. You are responsible. I know you save every penny you make at the library so that you can go to school. But what does Hannah do with her time? Frankly, I don't know."

"She's a complex person. Give her time."

Mr. Spelling. "Time to do what? Get even more off track?"

Mary was not sure what to say. "I just know that she's my friend. And that I think she'll turn out fine."

Mr. Spelling sat at his desk, wanting to get down to business. "Give me the facts of your record."

Mary spoke softly. "I have a three point seven five GPA. I got an eleven hundred and fifty on the SAT."

"The average student at Stanford practically got straight A's in high school. The average SAT is well over thirteen hundred."

Mary gulped. "I know that."

"What has Dick told you about my relationship with the university's chancellor?"

"He said you were good friends."

"We are not good friends. We are past business associates. There is a profound difference. If I ask him for a favor, I have to give him a favor in return." Mr. Spelling chewed on the situation for a moment, then he sighed. "I know this means a lot to you," he said finally.

"It means everything to me," Mary spoke sincerely. "But I don't want to put you on the spot, Mr. Spelling. I would appreciate anything you can do. But if I don't get in, I won't blame you. It will be my fault for not doing as well as Dick these past four years."

There was an awkward moment of silence. Then Mr. Spelling abruptly stood and offered his hand. "I appreciate that, Mary. Let's see what happens."

She shook his hand and left feeling that he would do nothing for her.

The night of the Sadie Hawkins dance, Mary tried to dress as if she were someone else. Unfortunately it wasn't a costume ball, and by the time Dick arrived she still looked like herself. A dozen times she second guessed herself about telling Charlie what she was up to, but she honestly decided he wouldn't hear about her date. He talked to a total of three people at school on a regular basis, and she was one of them. And if he did learn of her being with Dick, she figured she'd just tell him the whole story then.

But that wasn't a story she looked forward to relating. The more time she spent with Charlie, the more she realized how possessive he was. His casual demeanor hid a number of insecurities. Of course, she was no one to talk. If he went out with someone else, she would have thrown a fit. And she didn't see his clinging as a negative quality, but rather, as a sign of his devotion to her. So she didn't start out her date with Dick feeling relaxed and happy—anything but.

The dance was formal. Dick met her at her front door wearing a high-collared black and white tux that needed no tie. Mary wore a long green dress that her mother had copied from a picture on a magazine cover. Her parents didn't seem to mind that she was going with Dick instead of Charlie, although she had sworn them to secrecy. They liked Charlie, but maybe they liked Dick's money better.

"You look like a fox," Dick said when they were safely enclosed in his pearl white BMW. He leaned over to give her a kiss on the cheek and she pulled back.

"Don't get any ideas," she said.

He smiled. "You're in a friendly mood."

"You know my conditions. We're going out as friends."

"So I'm friendly."

She gestured to the steering wheel. "Drive, we'll be late. And don't try to kiss me at the dance."

He was curious. "What will you do if I try?"

"Something unpleasant," she said.

The dance was in the ballroom of Maple's one and only decent hotel. The place was jammed as they walked in and Mary cowered. Everyone was checking to see who Big Time Dick had brought, and she even thought she heard Charlie's name being whispered. But perhaps it was only her imagination because as they settled and started talking to people, no one asked her about Charlie. Dick was charming as usual. Everyone liked him except those who knew him well. But wasn't that the same with politicians everywhere? Mary could see Dick running for important offices in the future.

They danced; they ate from the buffet; they drank too much punch. On the whole it was a nice evening. Toward the end Mary began to relax fully. Her only regret was that Hannah was nowhere in sight, even though she'd said she'd be there. Mary asked Dick about his sister but he brushed the question off.

Out in the parking lot, when they were leaving to go home, Dick suddenly grabbed her and started kissing her hard. His timing could have been worse, however. Luckily they were one of the last couples to leave, and there was no one in sight. Still, she didn't like being attacked. Twice she pushed him off only to have him keep coming at her. Finally she slapped him across the face. He stopped and held his hand to his cheek as if she had shot him. She did have a strong arm, and there may have been blood on his lip. Even in the dark she could see the red in his blue eyes.

"What did you do that for?" he demanded.

"You have a lot of nerve," she swore quietly, checking around and seeing no one. "This is a casual date, I've told you a thousand times. I don't need your tongue in my mouth."

"I thought you wanted me to kiss you."

"Whatever gave you that idea?" she asked.

"The way you kept looking at me all night."

"I just looked at you. You weren't turning me on for godsakes."

"I think you liked it."

She opened the passenger door. "Take me straight home."

He slowly opened his door. "I thought you wanted to get a snack?"

"That was ten minutes ago. Really, Dick, you're impossible."

His voice had an edge to it. "No, Mary. I just think anything is possible."

He made another move on her in the car just outside her house. She couldn't believe his nerve, or his strength. This time he practically pinned her to the seat as he tried to kiss her. She thought he must be high on something but she didn't smell alcohol on his breath. This time she had to slug him in the throat to get him off. To her amazement he cocked his fist back, ready to take her head off. He was pissed, and she was really scared.

"Hit me and I'll scream," she hissed.

He paused. "You wouldn't dare."

She glanced at her house. There was a light on, her mom was waiting up for her. "It's you who wouldn't dare," she said softly.

He relaxed his hand and stared down the street. "You're never going to get into Stanford," he whispered.

"If sleeping with you is what it takes, I'd rather repeat high school." She opened the car door. "Thanks for the horrible evening."

He grabbed her arm and caught her eye. "Don't talk about tonight. To anyone. Understand?"

She held his eye. "You don't talk about tonight, I won't talk about it."

"Agreed."

She shook off his arm. "And don't even look at me at school. I don't want to have to see you."

Dick grinned. "You'll be back, Mary. You want it as much as I do."

It was all she could do not to spit in his face.

She got out of the car and slammed the door.

The next day the world ended. Charlie called her and told her to come over. It was an order, and not a friendly one. When she got to his house he was sitting on his front porch lighting wooden matches and letting them burn down low. She sat next to him for five minutes before she had the nerve to say anything. It wasn't as if he'd look at her. She couldn't understand how he'd found out so fast. It must have been Dick, she thought. Dick the bastard. He had probably called Charlie in the middle of the night to tell him how he had boinked their mutual love.

"I'd like to talk about it," she said finally.

He stared at a flame that was on the verge of licking his thumbnail.

"There's nothing to talk about," he muttered.

"It's not what you think," she said.

The flame died between his fingers. It must have hurt, but if it did Charlie gave no sign. He smiled as he snorted. He finally looked at her and she hardly recognized him.

"You don't know what I think, Mary," he said.

Her lower lip trembled. "I didn't go out with him to go out with him. Dick's father is a friend of Stanford's chancellor. Dick told me if I'd go with him to Sadie Hawkins, he would persuade his father to put in a good word for me."

Charlie stared at her with strange eyes. "I know you screwed him."

Mary sucked in a breath. "Who told you that?"

"It's all over town."

"Charlie! How can you say such a thing!"

He jumped up and glared down at her. "You cheated on me! You told me you had to study last night! You lied to me!"

She got up and forced herself to speak in an even tone.

"I did lie to you and I'm sorry for that," she said. "But you must know I have absolutely no romantic interest in Dick."

He was bitter. "Then why were you making out with him in the parking lot? Don't deny it."

"I wasn't making out with him. He forced himself on me. He attacked me." She tried to touch him. "Charlie. You have to believe me. I didn't sleep with him. I don't even like him."

He brushed her hand away and stared at the ground.

"I never want to see you again," he said quietly.

Tears stung her eyes. "Why?" she asked desperately. "Because I made a simple mistake? Because I just want to get into college? Are you going to condemn me because of that? Charlie, look at me. Tell me you forgive me."

He did look at her, but his face was not something she wanted to see. His jealousy had transformed him into a demon. His next words moved like a pitchfork through her guts.

"I never want to see you again because you're a whore," he said.

Then he walked away. From his own house. From his own true love. And all she could do was stand there and feel the pain.

By the time she was sitting with Hannah in Day Glow Donuts that night she was as angry as she was hurt. For ten minutes her friend listened to her spew out tears and threats, and still Mary showed no sign of slowing down. Hannah listened closely with a cigarette in her hand and a cloud of smoke hanging over her head.

"He didn't even give me a chance to explain," Mary said for the tenth time. "He just called me a whore and walked away. Can you believe that?"

"He's a guy," Hannah said. "I believe it."

Mary shook her head. "We've made love. We've slept together naked in the same bed. We've been as close as two people can be. I've told him my deepest dreams. He's shared with me the hopes he has for the future. Now I make one little mistake and I go from being the greatest thing in the world to a whore. Can you believe that?"

"Yes."

Mary sipped her coffee and then pounded the table. "I hate him! I want to kill him!" Then she lowered her head and burst out crying. "How can he do this to me? I love him, Hannah, I really do. You don't do this to someone you love."

"Did he ever say he loved you?" Hannah asked.

Mary looked up. "What?"

"Did he ever say he loved you? I mean, I know you say you loved him. But I don't see any sign that Charlie felt the same way about you."

Mary was taken aback. "He loves me. Or he did, I know he did." She wiped at her face. "When we slept together it was wonderful. He gave me so much love."

"When you slept together he gave you so much pleasure, and vice versa. Mary, a guy doesn't have to love you to sleep with you. You're eighteen, you should know that by now."

Mary stared at her a moment and then shook her head. "You don't understand. Charlie and me—we were *really* close. When we were together it was like magic."

Hannah tapped her cigarette and smiled.

"This magic doesn't sound that long lasting." After a pause she added, "But I do feel like you do. I feel he never gave you a chance to explain."

"He didn't," Mary said. "I wonder how he found out so fast?"

"That's a stupid question. I heard half the school was at the dance. Anyone could have told him. And while I'm on the subject, you were a fool to think he wouldn't find out." Hannah puffed on her Marlboro. "You know for a smart girl you do the dumbest things."

Mary continued to rub her eyes. "What am I going to do?"

"Do? You can't do anything. You just have to let it go."

Mary lowered her hands. "I can't. I love him."

"I thought you hated him?"

"I do hate him! He called me a whore! And the only person in the whole world I've slept with is him! God, I want to kill the bastard!"

"Lower your voice. People are listening."

Mary put a hand to her face and sighed. "I don't give a damn. About anything." Then she was crying again. "God, I love him and he calls me that. I tell you I can't stand this."

"Don't get mad, don't get sad." Hannah blew more smoke. "Get even."

Mary raised her eyes to Hannah's, showing interest. "What do you mean?"

"I have an idea."

"What kind of idea?"

Hannah slowly smiled. "A revenge kind of idea."

7

Deputy Howard was waiting when the four of them—Lieutenant Riles, Lieutenant Sharp, Mary, and Hannah—arrived at the Crossroads. But they no sooner arrived than the deputy left. He told them he was cold, and after both lieutenants congratulated him on his excellent work, they dismissed him.

The four of them walked toward the gun.

Both cops carried flashlights. The twin beams sparkled on the snow.

It was a silver revolver with a black butt and a four-inch barrel. Deputy Howard spotted it two hundred yards from where he had discovered the body, in the trees behind a cluster of bushes, in an inch of snow. He performed this remarkable detecting feat by following two sets of footprints to within yards of the gun. Footprints that led away from where Dick had been lying with his blood leaking onto the snow.

The deputy hadn't touched the weapon, so Riles carefully donned gloves and picked it up by the tip of the barrel. The two officers studied the chambers. There were six of them, with bullets in only two. But there were faint dark powder marks on the remaining chambers. The cops looked at each other. The two girls stood nearby, watching. Sharp spoke first, quietly, just to his partner.

"We don't know if it was fully loaded," he said. "The powder marks could have been from another time."

Riles shook his head, his eyes on the girls the whole time. They couldn't hear his whispered reply. "The marks are all identical. I think this gun was clean before it was fired tonight." He paused. "I think it was fired four times."

"But Kohner thought Dick had been shot at point blank range," Sharp said. "How could the person miss the first three times?"

"He could have been farther away when he first opened fire."

"I don't think so."

Riles shrugged. He stepped toward the girls and held the gun up for them to see. He shined his flashlight on it for effect. The girls cowered at the sight of it. Maybe a sign that they had seen it before? Riles held it so that it was only inches from their trembling faces. It was cold, this long winter night, only a short time until dawn. Riles spoke, "Have either of you seen this gun before?"

"No," Hannah said.

Mary shook her head and stared down at her feet.

"This is a three fifty-seven magnum," Riles said. "It shoots either three fifty-sevens—a powerful round—or ordinary thirty-eights. This gun fires six rounds. There are two rounds in it now—thirty-eights. Somebody most have fired off the other four rounds. Now Dick was shot with a hollow point thirty-eight. Chances are—since his body was found near here—that he was shot with this gun. We already know that Charlie's dad owned a gun like this. Chances are this is his. We'll be able to confirm that once we get back to town. After we study the gun, we'll be able to confirm many facts." He paused and his eyes bore into each of them. "Are you sure neither of you has seen this gun before?"

"I've never seen it before," Hannah said, and there was a note of defiance in her voice. She glanced over at Mary, who was still staring down in the direction of China.

"I don't know anything about this gun," Mary muttered. "Can we go home?"

"Not yet," Sharp said, standing beside his partner.

Hannah was angry. "You have no right to keep us. My father told you that at the station. You have to arrest us to hold us."

Mary raised her head and gave her a quick look that spoke clearly. *Shut your mouth and don't give them any ideas about arresting us.* But Hannah ignored her. Sharp gestured back the way they had come, where they had parked their car.

"We want to study the spot where we found your brother, Hannah," he said, and there was a gentleness in his voice. "If that would be all right with you?"

Hannah hesitated. "I'd rather not look at the spot if you don't mind."

"Will you come with us?" Riles asked Mary.

Mary touched her cold face with her gloved hands. It was almost as if she thought her skin were made of porcelain, and might break at any moment. She nodded her head slowly.

"If you want," she said quietly.

Dick had been found lying on his back, staring up at the sky, his eyeballs frozen, but *not* the rest of him. He hadn't been lying there all that long before he was discovered on a routine swing through the woods. Otherwise, in the zero temperatures, his whole body would have been stiff as—well, as stiff as a corpse.

Both Riles and Sharp knelt in the snow by the bloody spot, the red liquid frozen in a body-shaped depression like drippings from a meat locker. Hannah stood off to the left by the patrol car but Mary hovered nearby, her arms clasped across her chest. She kept moving to keep out the cold, or maybe it was because she was nervous. Riles frowned as he studied the frozen blood.

"There isn't much here," he said.

"I was thinking the same thing," Sharp said.

"He should have bled more. For godsakes, he was shot through the head. There should be blood all over this snow."

"But he died instantly. His heart stopped immediately." Sharp paused. "We could be wrong. We might want to bring Kohner out here."

"We'll bring him out tomorrow. This snow—or the blood—isn't going to melt in the next twenty-four hours." Riles glanced up at Mary, who didn't appear to be listening. He cleared his throat and spoke to her. "I don't think your friend was killed here. What do you think of that?"

Mary was very pale as she glanced at him. "I don't know what you mean."

Riles stood. "I think he was killed somewhere else, and his body was dumped here. Would you know anything about that?"

"No," Mary said. She glanced at Hannah, who was smoking a cigarette and staring at the sky. Riles took a step toward Mary with Sharp at his back.

"You look scared, Mary," Riles said. "Something special bothering you?"

'No."

"Are you sure?" Riles asked.

"No." Mary paused. "Yeah, this place. I hate this place. Can we go now?"

Sharp spoke in a soft soothing tone. "You can talk to us, Mary. Hannah can't hear us here. If you have something you want to tell us, tell us now."

Mary went back to searching for China. "I've told you everything I know."

"Are you sure?" Riles asked. "The last time you saw Dick he was sitting in his car—alone—at midnight?"

Mary looked up, nodded. "That's what I said."

"Where was Charlie at midnight?" Sharp asked.

"I don't know," Mary said. "I told you I didn't know."

Riles took another step closer. He was practically in her face. "Who are you protecting, Mary? Charlie? Hannah? Do you think they'll bother protecting you when the truth of what happened here comes out?"

Mary seemed to be having trouble breathing, but then she controlled herself. "I'm not protecting anyone," she whispered.

"I don't believe it," Riles said, glaring at her.

The three of them walked back toward the car, toward Hannah. But along the way Riles suddenly stopped and pointed to car tracks that led away from the Crossroads in the direction of Whistler, a neighboring town. Sharp followed Riles as he raised an arm and pointed.

"What are you thinking?" Sharp asked.

"That somebody who was out here tonight went to Whistler. Or at least started in that direction." Riles stepped to where both Mary and Hannah could hear him. He pointed out the tire tracks to the girls. There were several sets that overlapped in the snow. "Did any of you drive down this road tonight?" he asked.

"No," the girls said together, a shade too quickly Riles thought. He almost laughed out loud as he turned to his partner.

"We're definitely checking out this road," Riles said.

Mary appeared worried as Hannah stepped forward.

"Not with us you're not," Hannah said with strength. "Either you take us back to town right now or you arrest us."

Riles peered at Hannah through his frosty breath. Sharp came up behind his partner and put a hand on his shoulder. Sharp was concerned but Riles seemed past that point.

"We don't have enough evidence to arrest them," Sharp whispered in his ear.

"I don't care," Riles said. "I'm tired of this charade."

"They'll be out before the sun is up," Sharp warned.

"A lot can happen between now and then." Riles turned toward the car and nodded to Sharp. "Read them their rights. Then we take a drive up this road."

Sharp did as he was told. The girls were under arrest.

Hannah just snickered. Mary looked as if she wanted to kill her friend.

They took a drive on the road that led to Whistler. Sharp drove to the side of the tracks, trying not to disturb them. But the road was narrow and he failed miserably. Riles leaned out the window, his flashlight bouncing off the trees, the road, the snow. They had driven perhaps ten minutes when he motioned Sharp to stop.

"What is it?" Sharp asked.

"Turn off the engine; we're getting out," Riles said as he opened his door.

Off to the right side of the road, beside a bush, was another pool of frozen blood. This one was larger than the other. It looked as if someone had lost at least a pint, if not twice that. Riles kept his light focused on it as he knelt beside the dark ice. He nodded grimly.

"I think we've discovered where Dick really died," he said.

Sharp wasn't sure. "We'll have to take a sample of this blood to compare to the other. I have plastic bags in the trunk. Kohner can type them right away."

Riles glanced at the girls, who hadn't gotten out of the car. Mary had rolled down her window, however.

"How does it feel to be under arrest for murder?" Riles asked casually.

"We didn't do anything," Mary muttered, although she seemed worried about the stain on the road. She pointed. "What's that?"

"I'll give you one good guess," Riles said as he stood. He spoke to his partner. "Take your sample. We'll get another sample from the other site on the way back." He turned. "I want to look around a bit, before anyone else gets out here."

Riles found another frozen blood puddle a few seconds later, not twenty feet up the road. This one was larger than the first, but not so large as the second. Still, whoever had made it had lost a lot of blood. The big question was if it had all come from the same person.

"The body must have been moved a few times," Sharp said.

"No way," Riles said. "There would be bloody tracks connecting the puddles."

"Not if someone wrapped his head."

"If they wrapped his head once we wouldn't have so many puddles. No, I think we're going to discover that these blood samples don't all match."

Sharp considered. "You think Charlie died here as well?"

"Yeah. I do."

"But he's our main suspect," Sharp protested.

"Not if he's dead he isn't," Riles said. "I'm telling you, somebody fired that gun four times."

"Maybe," Sharp said and then lowered his voice. "I still think you overplayed our hand by arresting the girls. Judge Pierce will give them bail in five seconds. And you know Hannah's father is going to wake the old goat up the moment we get back to town. The two play golf together all summer."

Riles was smiling. He nodded to shoe prints in the snow beside the last puddle of frozen blood. There were a variety of shapes, each captured in a solid mold of ice.

"Get the girls out here," he said. "I want to check the imprints of their sneakers."

Sharp turned the car headlights back on while the girls stood shivering not far from the tracks around the third puddle. It was only here that there were clear tracks. The rest of the snow was too messed up. Riles got down on his hands and knees and told the girls to each raise a foot. Mary did so without complaining but Hannah was tired of taking orders.

"You have no right to do this," she said. "I want to talk to a lawyer."

"When we get back to town," Riles muttered. "You can talk to the President of the United States for all I care. But for right now you're going to raise your shoe so that I can study the bottom of it."

Hannah started to say something but then thought better of it. She lifted her foot partway so that Riles practically had to lay his cheek on the snow to see the sole. He didn't seem to mind because a grin broke out across his face. He stood suddenly and spoke to Sharp, who was still collecting a blood sample.

"Mary is wearing New Balance running shoes," Riles said. "Hannah has on Nike walking shoes. Guess what kind of shoe imprints we have around puddle number three?"

"New Balance and Nike's?" Sharp asked.

"Yes. Isn't that amazing?" Riles turned back to the girls. "If either of you wants to change your story now's the time. But let me warn you, lie to us again and the court will take that into account when deciding what to do with you two."

Mary acted as if she wanted to speak, but Hannah cut her off sharply with a gesture and her voice. Sharp wandered over to see yet another confrontation between the girls and Riles.

"Lots of people wear Nikes and New Balance," Hannah said, as much for Mary's benefit as for the cops'. "It proves nothing. I know the law. You'd have to match our DNA with some of the blood you found here to prove that we had definitely been here. That will never happen." She turned to her friend. "Mary, we have the right to remain silent. Don't say anything else to these cops until you talk to my father's lawyer. They'll just use it against you."

Riles spoke to his friend. "Handcuff these young women. And while you're at it, put plastic bags over each of their hands. When we get back to town I want to check their skin for powder marks." Riles stepped close to Hannah and breathed frost in her face. "Did you wash your hands tonight, Hannah? Did you wash them real well?"

Hannah did not seem scared at all. "I guess we'll find out, won't we?"

8

It was the night of the murder. But no one was supposed to die, Mary had understood. They were just supposed to scare Charlie. Scare him out of his pants so he'd feel bad about everything he had done to Mary. And then . . . then he was supposed to want her back. In Mary's mind, even then, this one and one did not add up to two. Mary knew she was dealing in fractions of reality. Charlie was two dimensional, and he couldn't possibly conform to her simple equation. Still, she was so mad at him she didn't really care if he did or didn't.

And that was as untrue as anything could possibly be.

They were Mary, Hannah, and Dick.

They were sitting in the Pizza Palace eating—what else—pizza. The time was between nine and ten. So later, what Mary told Riles and Sharp was true. But just the first part. Charlie had never been to the Pizza Palace that night. He was supposed to meet Mary at twelve midnight at the Crossroads, as far as Mary knew. She had called him and asked him to meet her. They were going to *talk* out their problems. He had agreed to come, and she had been surprised.

"Charlie wanted to know why the hell we had to meet out there," Mary said to Dick and Hannah. They were sitting in a booth in the corner. The place was crowded and loud; it was all the town had going on Friday night. Mary kept glancing around to see if anyone she knew was there, and, lo and behold, she realized she knew everyone. She was pissed at Hannah for talking her into such a stupid plan. And it was stupid, there was no debating that.

"That doesn't matter," Hannah said, blowing smoke.

"One place is as good as another," Dick said.

Mary chewed on cold crust. "I don't know why we're doing this."

"We don't have to do it," Dick said.

"Shut up," Hannah said.

Dick shrugged. "He's such an ape. How do I know he won't attack me?"

"Because you'll be the one with the gun, stupid," Hannah said.

Dick gave a weird grin and looked at Mary. "And what do I get out of all this?"

"The thrill of the scare," Hannah said.

"I want sex," Dick said flatly.

"Subtle, aren't we?" Mary said.

Dick drank his beer. He was, of course, underage but that didn't seem to matter in Maple. "I tried subtlety and it didn't work," he said.

"Sticking your tongue in my mouth was not subtle," Mary said. She threw her pizza crust aside and leaned closer. "Do this tonight and get me into Stanford, and then you get some of what you want."

Dick was amused. "The hookers in Vegas aren't as pricey as this."

"But you don't want a hooker," Mary said.

Dick snorted. "Isn't that what I'm getting?"

Mary started to slap him. Hannah caught her hand midflight.

"Why are you so interested in her body, anyway?" Hannah asked her brother, putting Mary's hand back in its proper place, or almost.

Dick eyed her and it seemed a familiar inspection. "For the same reasons you are, sis."

Mary blinked. "Am I missing something?"

She realized right then that she was. Her hand was on Hannah's knee. She quickly took it off.

Hannah didn't care. "You take care of your end and I'm sure Mary will take care of hers."

"Where did you get the gun?" Mary asked Dick.

Dick was looking out the window. "Does it matter? I have one, a revolver, and I have blanks as well."

"Are you absolutely sure they're blanks?" Mary asked for the second time. She had no idea where Dick or anyone could possibly buy such things.

Dick stared out the window and contemplated the external darkness. "They're blanks," he finally answered. "They won't even scratch your pretty boy."

"We assume you tested them on yourself," Hannah said.

Dick burped. "That's right."

Mary shook her head. "This plan is no plan at all. It is totally unsophisticated. I'm supposed to meet Charlie in the woods and then you're going to jump out from behind a tree and start shooting. I mean, what the hell kind of plan is that?"

"I'm not going to sit out there in the cold and wait for you guys," Dick said. "I'm going to drive up shooting."

Mary was disgusted. "That's even worse. That really won't work."

"We're not planning a bank robbery," Hannah said. "We want Charlie to piss his pants. It's better to keep it simple and stupid. Believe me, when Dick starts firing Charlie will start running."

"Then what?" Mary asked.

Hannah stubbed out her cigarette in the cold crust. "Then you can start laughing your head off, who cares? Then you tell Charlie he's been an asshole and you make love and make up."

"In that order?" Mary asked.

"What are you bitching about?" Hannah asked. "I'm doing you a favor. You said you wanted to kill the guy."

"I think we should kill him," Dick muttered.

Mary put her hand to her head and groaned. "I feel like I'm getting in over my head."

Hannah lit another cigarette, holding it in her left hand. "You're a lightweight, this is nothing."

Dick was suddenly concerned. "Charlie could go to the police and report me."

Hannah waved her hand. "He'll be too embarrassed when he realizes they were just blanks."

"Charlie is no fan of the police," Mary muttered. "You don't have to worry about that."

"Do I have to worry about the terms of collection?" Dick asked.

Mary fidgeted. "You're despicable."

Dick was happy again. "You can close your eyes and pretend it's Charlie."

Mary growled. "Scaring Charlie is secondary to getting me into Stanford."

"Then you can pay me back on the installment plan," Dick said.

Mary stared at him and realized with sudden clarity that she would never sleep with him, no matter what he did for her. Of course, once she was accepted at Stanford it would be hard for them to unaccept her. Dick wanted her so bad that he didn't know how stupid he was being.

"Payment is only made upon full delivery," she said to him.

He looked at her as if he knew what she was thinking. Maybe he did; maybe he didn't care. He stood suddenly and thrust his hands deep in his coat pockets. Something was buried in there, maybe it was the gun. Again she wondered where he would have bought blanks.

"I'm going to the movies," Dick said abruptly.

Hannah was annoyed. "You don't have time for a movie. You have to be at the Crossroads at exactly twelve-ten."

"The movie is over at twenty to twelve," he said. "I checked."

"What movie?" Hannah demanded. *"Ashes of Agony?* It started ten minutes ago. You can't go; it's not fair."

"I'm going; it's Friday night," Dick said, and walked away.

Hannah sprang out of her seat. "I'll talk to him, Mary. You stay here."

"I don't want to stay here," Mary said. She could taste the pizza in her throat and it was not inspiring. Hannah paused to stare at her. Mary wondered if she was looking at her in a sexual way. It was just a thought.

"I'll meet you in an hour in the center of the square," Hannah said finally.

"I don't like this," Mary said.

Hannah smiled. "You're going to love it."

An hour later, sitting in the center of the square, Mary chatted with Deputy Howard when he pulled up in his cruiser. He was not much older than she was—three years—but there was a sad inevitability about him that said he was already beat. Howard had a gut and bad heartburn and slouched when he thought he was standing tall. Seldom was his shirt tucked in all the way. His greatest hope for this particular incarnation was to be a good cop. Not that Mary had anything against cops, it was just that Howard would never be very good at that either. Howard was kind of slow, his brain was, and there was a clumsiness to his movements that made even strangers yawn. Married to the first girl he had ever slept with—the equally cerebral JoDean Jones—they had already made three little babies that cried all the time. When he was not being a deputy, he worked as a fryer at Harvey's, just to be able to feed the munchkins. Mary liked him, even though she felt sorry for him. He asked how she was doing, and they chatted about the weather and other such Howard-like subjects. Then he moved on in a black and white cruising the cold night.

Mary hoped he wouldn't hear the gunshots.

Yet she wished she had asked Howard where one bought blanks.

Hannah finally showed up and she was in a cheery mood.

"Dick is fine, he'll be there on time," Hannah said.

"I forgot to ask, where are you going to be at midnight?" Mary asked.

"I want to watch. I'll be in the woods, out of sight. Drop me off before you get to the Crossroads."

"Do you think that's wise?" Mary asked.

"What does wisdom have to do with any of this? Why are you in such a bad mood?"

"Because I don't like guns. I don't like any form of revenge. I don't know why I'm doing this."

Hannah knelt in front of Mary and brushed

her own blond hair back. The move was not necessary because Hannah had recently taken to wearing her hair shortish, sort of butchlike. Yet she wore thick red lipstick and mascara, odd. Hannah rested her elbows on Mary's knees.

"What are you thinking?" Hannah asked.

"I told you."

"Nah. You're wondering if I'm a lesbian."

"No." A pause. "Are you?" Mary asked.

"Does it matter?"

"No. Are you?"

Hannah considered seriously. "I don't know what I am. I think I'm bi." She paused. "Does that gross you out?"

"No. Not as long as you don't want to undress me."

Hannah was thoughtful, her unfocused gaze shifted to a distant point.

"I just want to do this to Charlie," she muttered.

"I love Charlie," Mary said.

Hannah appraised her. "Honestly? I don't think so, Mary."

"You don't know me."

"You don't know yourself. You don't know what you're capable of."

Mary stood. "I'm getting cold."

They got in the car, Mary's car, the one Charlie had fixed. They turned on the heat and drove around. They ran into Deputy Howard again—that part of what Mary later told Riles and Sharp was true. Yet it was the second time Mary had seen Howard that night, and the first time she had been alone when she was supposed to be with Hannah. These pesky details—they had buried wiser people than Mary and Hannah.

Closing on midnight, they drove toward the Crossroads. Two hundred yards from the spot, Mary slowed and let Hannah out. The snow was deep except under the still and silent trees. Hannah wished her good luck. Mary thought it an odd remark. Alone, she drove to the Crossroads, parked, and got out. The chill from the snow went right through her running shoes, up her legs, into her chest even, where her heart strained to keep her body warm. What an idiot, she told herself, not to wear boots. She loved Charlie. Hannah was wrong. Hannah just wanted to seduce her.

In the distance Mary could see a truck approaching.

It looked like Charlie's.

9

Back at the police station, Lieutenant Riles and Lieutenant Sharp got one of their wishes fulfilled. They had taken a sample of Mary's damp hair and put it in a plastic Baggie. Through the clear bag they could see that the hair fibers had stained the plastic red. The police gave one another knowing looks. Sweet innocent Mary had blood on her hair.

But whose blood?

They gave the sample to Dr. Kohner, who was working very late, and asked him to type it immediately, along with the samples of blood from the frozen puddles. A definitive test, such as a DNA comparison, could take as much as a month to conduct. But typing the blood would narrow the number of suspects, and the two detectives believed that might be enough to make one of the girls talk. Obviously, they thought it would be Mary. Hannah had retreated to a slant-eyed realm of silent venom. Curious, since it was her beloved brother who had taken the slug in the eye.

Typing would take at least two hours, maybe three.

There was still no word on Charlie. Where he might be, what he might be breathing. Air or dirt, snow or water.

Outside, the sun slowly began to warm the sky.

The detectives placed the girls back in the interrogation room where Mary had spent a portion of the night. The police station wasn't that large; they used the room for taking physical evidence as well as verbal. After drawing the blood, the detectives called for the coroner. At first Kohner hung in the background, and to the girls, he looked like a healthy corpse come to feed on their brains. He stared at them as if he had energy left for another autopsy. He only stepped forward as Riles was preparing to sample the *stuff* under their nails, and the *stuff* on their hands, particularly around their thumbs, where powder remains from a fired revolver would collect. Riles, with Kohner's help, used needles, razors, and tweezers. They scraped the girl's skin very lightly, but Hannah hated the process and expressed her discomfort.

"You can't do this," she said. "I want to see my lawyer. I want to talk to my father."

"You can talk to both after we've collected our samples," Riles said, holding Hannah's hands firmly. "Remember, young lady, you are under arrest and charged with first degree murder."

Hannah snorted. "Not for long."

"We can keep you for at least twenty-four hours," Sharp said.

"We'll be out of here in less than four," Hannah answered.

That could be true, the cops thought. Hannah's father did know the judge and probably sent him expensive Christmas cards each year. But at least by then they'd have the blood typed. It was going to be real interesting to see what matched what. Riles could hardly wait to get the results, but Sharp was still uneasy. Hannah seemed awfully confident, as Mary showed signs of cracking.

Confident Hannah, not devastated Hannah.

She had tossed aside the charade of grief without realizing it.

"You have pretty hands," Kohner said to Mary as he scraped her skin carefully with the edge of his razor.

"Thank you," Mary said quietly.

Kohner leaned over and sniffed them. "But they smell like a strong cleaning solution. Do you use such a product to soften them or clean them?"

Mary stared. "Neither," she muttered.

Kohner turned to Riles. Sharp also came forward. The coroner seemed to want Riles's permission. Riles nodded, and the coroner leaned over to smell Hannah's hands. He sat back and smiled, but the detectives weren't sure they liked the joke.

"What is it?" Riles demanded.

"Smart girls," Kohner said. "They have both soaked their hands in what seems to be Lysol."

Riles was angry. "That wipes out any powder trace?"

"No," Kohner said. "Not definitively. But it makes it hard to find."

Riles glared at Hannah. "You think you're way ahead of us."

Hannah allowed a thin smile. "How much do cops make a year?"

The question was both insulting and incriminating. Hannah was now her father's only heir. Soon she would be filthy rich while they would still be grinding out miserable salaries. Really, she had a lot of guts to ask what she did. Riles had to restrain himself from slapping her, and he had never hit a woman in his life.

Right then Riles knew they had their murderer.

Yet Sharp was unsure, and Sharp was no dummy.

"It is not how much a person makes that matters," Riles said seriously. "It is how they earn it. Many of the richest people in the world are the most miserable. Especially when they have destroyed their humanity to get what they have." He glanced at Mary. "They have no peace of mind. Their consciences haunt them."

"You think I'm just a punk kid," Hannah said. "That I have no conscience."

Riles continued to look at Mary. "Did you soak your hands in Lysol?"

"I washed them at the gas station," Mary said. "I don't know what kind of stuff they had there."

"Which gas station?" Sharp asked.

"I can't remember," Mary said.

"Charlie hasn't shown up yet," Sharp said. "We've sent a squad car over to his house a dozen times." He paused. "Can you remember where he is?"

"No." A small syllable.

Riles turned to Kohner. "Do the powder stains on their skin anyway. We'll see what we get." The stain reacted with spent gunpowder. Even through heavy chemicals, it could still work.

Kohner nodded. "I have another interesting find on Dick's blood."

Riles wanted the girls to hear. "What was it?" he said.

"Besides being drunk, Dick had PCP in his blood."

The information astounded Mary. She whirled on Hannah, and almost said words the cops would have paid dearly to hear. But at the last moment she restrained herself. The information caught Riles offguard as well. PCP, or angel dust, was one of the few street drugs that made users aggressive. Yet in Maple and the surrounding area PCP was almost unknown. And it was an awfully heavy-duty chemical for a student body president to be snorting.

"Did Dick do PCP?" Riles asked Hannah.

Hannah shrugged. "He did different drugs, I'm not sure which."

"Where did he get his drugs?" Sharp asked.

"I don't know," Hannah said.

Sharp frowned. "This doesn't fit."

"Maybe it does," Riles said, watching Hannah. She met his gaze.

"Enough of this playing Sherlock Holmes," she said. "I want to make one phone call. I'm allowed that, ain't I, even though I am under arrest?"

"Your father is still waiting outside," Riles said.

"Good," Hannah said sarcastically. "Then I can call him on his cell phone."

The detectives told her to wait a minute and retreated into the hallway for still another conference. Kohner followed them, wishing he were a detective on this exciting night. He had a gleam in his eyes.

"Why did you reveal all that stuff in front of them?" Sharp asked his partner.

"I was trying to rattle them," Riles said.

"We're the ones who're getting rattled," Sharp complained. He spoke to Kohner, "How much PCP did Dick have in his system?"

"A lot."

"On top of the alcohol?" Sharp said.

Kohner considered. "It would not be precise or professional of me to say the molecules of alcohol were on top of the PCP molecules. But as a layman I can answer your question in the affirmative."

"He was stoned out of his mind then," Sharp said. "He didn't know what he was doing."

"Maybe someone wanted him that way," Riles mused.

"You're thinking of her salary comment," Sharp said. "I think you're reading too much into it. I mean, he was her brother for godsakes—her twin. She's only eighteen—how could she shoot her own brother?"

"She certainly didn't spend a long time mourning her twin," Riles muttered. "We can't let them go before we at least have a report back on the blood."

Mr. Spelling accosted them next. No one had invited him back into the rear of the station—he made his own way. He still looked shaken, but he was mad again as well.

"Where's my daughter?" he demanded. "I've been here all night."

Riles took the heat. "She's under arrest," he said.

Mr. Spelling didn't get it. "What? What for?"

Riles spoke seriously. "For the murder of Richard Spelling, your son. Mary Dammon is under arrest as well."

Mr. Spelling's bull neck seemed to swell. "That is the most ridiculous thing I have heard in my life. You let me see Hannah and you let me see her right now."

"You can see your daughter," Riles said. "Later. But she doesn't leave here unless she is granted bail by the judge."

Mr. Spelling gave Riles the evil eye. He could have had a devil in his eyeball because it looked as if some tiny demon was pushing from the inside out.

"You are history, detective. For you to add to our sorrow at this time goes beyond forgiveness." Spelling held up a shaking finger. "This is the end of your career. It finishes tonight. You won't get away with this, I promise."

Sharp moved close to his partner. "We have strong circumstantial evidence for arresting your daughter and Mary. If you'll give us a few minutes, and stop threatening us, we can explain it to you. We all want the same thing here—to find the murderer of your son."

Mr. Spelling's face shook with fury. "By arresting Hannah? How can you be that sick?"

"Your daughter has lied to us all night," Mr. Riles said firmly. "You can see her later, and you can ask her about those lies. But as I said, she doesn't leave here until and unless she's granted bail. Now get back out to the waiting room and stay there until we call you."

Riles had his own power. Mr. Spelling turned and left.

Sharp groaned. "How come we're not loved like cops on TV?"

"Because they're usually continuing characters," Riles muttered.

"I'll be happy to testify at your job dismissal trial that you both behaved in the most professional of manners," Kohner said.

Riles was weary. "Will it be as much fun as an autopsy?"

"Very similar, I believe," Kohner said.

Riles was not looking forward to what he

had to do next. He had to get Judge Pierce on the phone before Spelling got to him. Spelling might go to the judge even before he called a lawyer. Riles hurried into his office, Sharp on his tail, and looked up the number on his computer. It rang a few times before the judge answered.

"This had better be good," Pierce mumbled. He was close to seventy and made of stone. He took a five-mile walk every afternoon and had a brisk voice. Ordinarily, without the Spelling connection, Riles would not have minded Pierce's involvement with the case. The judge had a shrewd legal mind and was not intimidated in the courtroom. He never, in Riles's memory, came to a decision just because it was politically correct. Yet Sharp was right, they didn't have enough evidence to hold the girls and Pierce would quickly grasp that. Then, when Spelling got to him, they'd have trouble holding the girls at all. Pierce was honest but not stupid. Spelling owned half the town and a hundred percent of the mayor. Riles knew the latter would be calling next, as soon as he woke up and heard the news.

"Eighteen-year-old Richard Spelling was murdered last night," Riles said.

Pierce had to take a breath. "Tell me."

Riles gave him an overview and then

dropped the bomb concerning the girls' arrests. Riles, in explaining why he moved so quickly, pushed hard on the girls' lousy attitudes. It was a mistake with Pierce. He wanted facts, not cop psychology.

"The soles of the shoes match perfectly," Riles repeated when he felt he was losing the judge. "They were there, I'm sure of it, and that's where Dick must have died."

"You're not sure where Dick died," Pierce corrected him. "But even if you are right about that, the shoe prints alone aren't enough to tie the girls to the scene of the crime."

"The prints also matched their shoe sizes."

"But as your partner no doubt told you, all kids wear those same shoes in about the same size."

"Sharp agreed with my decision to arrest," Riles said. Sitting across from him, Sharp nodded. They stuck together, in good and bad. But of the two of them only Riles knew how bad this could be if they screwed up.

Pierce continued. "I respect you, lieutenant, I always have. I know you must have had a long and trying night. And you have collected several pieces of interesting evidence. But, in my opinion, you have failed to make a case for why the girls were arrested tonight. In two or three days, *if* they were at the scene of the crime, you should have far more evidence. Better to use science than inspiration. Call the state police, get their experts out."

"I have already spoken to the state police. I know how to handle a homicide. But I must protest a couple of your remarks, your honor. I wouldn't have got the blood from Mary's hair if I hadn't arrested them. These girls may only be eighteen, but they're both strong willed and smart. That Hannah—if I didn't know better I'd have thought she already went to law school, or worse, was a part-time cop."

"I know Hannah." There was a dead spot on the line. "I'm getting another call."

"Don't take it," Riles said quickly. "It's Spelling." He almost added "please" but knew that would backfire with Pierce. In either case, the judge ignored the call.

"Dick was everything to his father," Pierce said with a sigh. "What can I say to him? He'll want his daughter at home at a time like this."

"We can't let them go until we get the blood types back."

"What are you looking for with the blood?"

"A link, of course."

"Have you got their blood types on file?"

"I'm running that down now," Riles lied.

"What if Mary has Charlie's blood in her hair and not Dick's?"

"I've wondered that myself, your honor. But any way you look at it that is still a link."

118

"Not until you find Charlie's body," Pierce said.

"He might be dead, you know. Personally I think he is."

"Why get rid of one body and not the other?"

"To make it look like Charlie did it and then fled."

Pierce considered. This was the bad part, his legal mind filing through previous cases. When it came down to it, Riles thought, the law had been designed for the guilty—not for the dead. They never got to file an appeal.

"The only way we can hold these girls is if the blood in Mary's hair matches Dick's," Pierce said finally. "Otherwise we have to let them go. How much more time do you need?"

"Three hours."

"It's six-thirty now. You have till ten."

"What will you set bail at?"

"Does it matter in Hannah's case?"

"No, I suppose not." Riles paused. Spelling could pay anything. "I'd still like to hold Mary."

"Why? There's time, lieutenant. Build your case slowly and methodically."

Riles felt a chill creep through his body. "Your honor, honestly, I don't know how much time there is." He added, "It might be good to hold Mary for her own protection."

"Try explaining that to her. Or to her lawyer."

"Spelling will not hire an attorney for Mary. He'll see the conflict of interest right away."

Pierce sharpened his tone. "It doesn't matter. Mary has to have Dick's blood on her or she walks. Her family is not rich, and they've lived here forever so her bail will not be excessive."

Riles realized the conversation was in effect over. They exchanged goodbyes. Riles told Sharp the details, which felt ominous to Riles. He tried to explain his bad vibes to his partner.

"Pierce could do nothing more for us under the circumstances," Sharp said.

Riles waved his hand. "It's not that. I expected no more from Pierce. I keep feeling that if we let these girls go more people could die."

Sharp shook his head. "Now you sound like a TV cop."

"There's something cold about that Hannah."

"Now Mary is innocent?" Sharp asked. "And Charlie?"

Riles felt as if he were missing something important. "You know, we haven't even sat down together and tried to figure out a scenario for what happened. For the sake of argument, let's say both girls are guilty. What exactly did they do? Why did they do it?"

"Speculating on what they did is easy. It's also a waste of time at this point. We'll come up with a dozen scenarios. Speculating on their motive is impossible. They have their whole lives in front of them and they're both smart girls. Why would they throw everything away so they could kill Dick?"

"And Charlie?" Riles said.

Sharp frowned. "If the girls are guilty—and that's still a hell of an *if* in my mind—then it's possible Charlie helped them kill Dick, and then fled so that he wouldn't have to take the heat."

Riles was doubtful. "Sounds reasonable, but it doesn't fit what we know. Mary is genuinely worried about Charlie, sorrowful even."

"But Hannah isn't," Sharp said.

"No. I tell you, Hannah is scary. She doesn't seem to feel anything except concern about being caught. Even there, she's cocky for an eighteen-year-old who's just been put under arrest. It's as if she has something secret up her sleeve that will make everything OK for her. One thing's for sure, though, Mary is angry at Hannah."

"I noticed that. Hannah is controlling Mary."

"Absolutely. And she has her on a tight leash."

"How?" Sharp asked.

"Fear. She gave Mary the story Mary gave us."

"How does the PCP in Dick's blood fit into all of this?" Sharp asked. "In front of the girls you acted like you knew."

"That was mostly show. But we're dealing with a crime of aggression and PCP is famous for making people aggressive."

"Your logic is circular," Sharp said. "You're saying Dick did do it then. He's the one with drugs in his veins."

"No. I mean there could be a connection here that we're missing. Maybe someone gave Dick the drugs without his knowledge."

"So he could shoot Charlie?"

"Possibly," Riles said.

"Then who shot Dick? The same person who drugged him?"

"Exactly," Riles said.

"You're reaching Steve."

Riles agreed. "I'm bent over backward and kissing my own ass. Maybe even the murderer's ass. That reminds me. I want to run down the medical records on Dick, Charlie, Mary, and Hannah. I told Pierce we'd done it already. We need those records to cross-type the blood samples. Then I want photos of the tracks out at the Crossroads, and the place past there, where the other blood puddles are. We need to secure those areas with live bodies. When the town wakes up, over half the local population will rush out to see where Dick died. When does Howard wake up?"

"He just went to bed. And I think he has his other job to go to today."

"Wake him up now. Tell him he's working for us for the next two days and no one else. Threaten to give him a promotion. Send him out to the Crossroads. In fact, on second thought, tell him to meet me there. I want to take the pictures. I have my camera in the car. That way I'll know they're done right." Riles stopped and rapped his office table lightly. "I need to give Pierce something stronger by ten o'clock or we lose the girls. For all I know, they'll go out and shoot each other."

"Maybe Charlie will show up and tell us his version of the story."

"Charlie's dead," Riles said, standing. "While I'm out there I'm going to look for his body."

Sharp also stood. "I'll run down the records. Do you plan on sleeping today?"

"No. You?"

Sharp smiled. "Since we both may be out of work by tomorrow I may as well put in one last hard day."

Riles eyed him. "It could come to that."

Sharp nodded. "Where you go I go."

"Even if it's in the wrong direction?"

Sharp patted him on the back. "No guts, no glory. You're taking chances, I probably should be doing the same. When do you want to meet?"

"In two hours. Here."

"To say goodbye to the girls?"

Riles groaned. "To wring their pretty necks. God, teenagers aren't what they used to be. When I was in high school it was only the guys who killed people."

"It's a sad world," Sharp said.

Riles didn't speak to anyone else before he left the station.

Riles was an amateur photographer. He hadn't been exaggerating when he said he was the best one to photograph the crime scene. He always carried his Nikon and several boxes of film in the trunk of his car. Even though the sun was filtered by a cover of clouds, he wasn't worried about the light. He knew enough about film speed and lens apertures to record exactly what he wanted.

Naturally he stopped first at the Crossroads, where Dick had been found. The scene had been contaminated by footprints, a problem almost impossible to avoid in snow. Working quickly, Riles shot the frozen blood puddle from various angles, and then shot the path to the gun. The two trails of footprints that led in the direction of the revolver matched the prints he had found at the other puddles: New Balance running shoes and Nike walking shoes. Pierce should be impressed, but Riles knew it wouldn't be enough.

There was no sign of Deputy Howard. Riles wrote a note for him and pinned it to a tree and then proceeded toward the second spot. He actually parked down the road from the puddles, trying to photograph the tire marks in the snow that led to the frozen blood. Of course these had also been contaminated from earlier swing bys. But he managed to get several clear shots of the tire tracks that had been there first. He was quite sure they would match Mary's tires.

Finally Riles photographed the two mysterious puddles. In his heart he was convinced that one belonged to Dick, the other to Charlie. He examined the latter, smaller puddle carefully. A faint trail of blood drops led away from it toward the first set of tire tracks and then stopped. They had picked up his body, Riles thought, and dumped it in the car trunk. Unless they had prepared the trunk ahead of time, there should be traces of blood in Mary's car still. He would check the vehicle before he went back in the station. By no coincidence, he had Mary's car keys in his pocket.

The original tire tracks continued deeper

into the woods, along the narrow road that led to Whistler. Riles was tempted to follow them but felt time was pressing. He had already spent ninety minutes taking pictures, fifteen rolls of film. Few laymen realized how exhausting homicide cases were. Documentation was everything. The state police would bring out their own people and duplicate his efforts, and then some. Judge Pierce did have a point. If the girls had been at the murder scene, they should be able to find a piece of definitive evidence. Riles's instincts were working overtime, and he knew Hannah still had plans Mary didn't even know about. He was sure of it.

Back at the Crossroads Riles found Deputy Howard dozing behind the wheel of his patrol car. Riles woke him roughly and told him to tape off the entire area. Howard complained that he didn't have enough tape and Riles told him to find some. Riles had hired Howard and felt it was his right to yell at him as often as Howard needed it. Yet he liked the slow-brained guy.

Back at the station, Riles went to Mary's car, an old Honda Civic, and opened the trunk. He slipped on a pair of latex gloves. It took him only a moment to spot the bottle of Lysol.

It was half-empty.

"Mary," he muttered as he photographed it

before removing it from the trunk. He searched the trunk carefully; Mary normally kept the space clean. Later the tech boys would go over it carefully but to his unaided eye there wasn't a sign of blood. There was, however, a half-used box of plastic garbage bags. Few items would have been more effective at containing blood spills. Riles muttered Mary's name again but this time he added a curse.

Inside the station, he found Kohner and Sharp sitting in his office. From the expressions on their faces, they had the results of the initial blood typing and the information wasn't good, or at least, not good for the case he was trying to build. For relatives of Mary and Hannah, the information might have been wonderful. Riles plopped down in his chair.

"Give it to me," he said.

"All of our young contestants have been treated at Maple Memorial at one point in their lives," Sharp said. "Their records are as follows: Dick is type A; Hannah is type B; Mary is type AB; and Charlie is a universal donor, type O. Because they are all different, the positive and negative RH factors are unimportant." Sharp paused. "Are you ready for this?"

Riles shrugged. "Sure."

Kohner spoke. "The first puddle of blood

you found at the Crossroads is type A. That must be from Dick. The second larger puddle you found closer to Whistler is also type A. So, you are right, Dick was probably killed there and then dumped at the Crossroads. The second puddle out there is type O. Again, you're probably right that it belongs to Charlie. They both must have died within moments of each other, certainly within a few feet of each other."

"What about the blood in Mary's hair?" Riles asked impatiently. That was what mattered most at the moment. Connecting at least one of the girls to the dead and the missing. Sharp and Kohner glanced at each other before Sharp answered.

"The blood on Mary's hair is type AB. She has a cut on her head. It seems to be nothing more than her own blood."

"Did you ask her how she got the cut?" Riles asked, feeling a sinking sickness in the pit of his stomach. There was no question—Pierce would have to let the girls go. Riles reflected on how unlucky they were; each of the people involved had a different blood type. The odds were against that, but not excessively so.

"She said she couldn't remember," Sharp replied.

"Naturally," Riles mumbled. He held up

the bottle of Lysol he had found. He still had his gloves on. "In the trunk of Mary's car."

"It's something," Sharp said.

"It ain't much," Riles growled. He turned to Kohner. "How did the stain on their skin go for powder marks?"

"I used only a fraction of our samples," Kohner said. "I'm sending the bulk of them out to private labs. They'll do a much better job than I can here. But they may not be able to get past the Lysol. I was unable to." He paused. "There's no *clear* sign of expelled powder on either of the girl's hands."

"Is there any sign?" Riles persisted.

"Yes," Kohner said. "But it's so faint and so compromised by the other chemicals, I doubt that it would be allowed in a court of law."

"Who had it on her hands?" Riles asked.

"Hannah," Kohner said. "On the left hand."

"Hannah is left handed," Riles said, remembering.

"It's another piece of the puzzle," Sharp said hopefully.

"Pierce is too old to play with puzzles," Riles said.

"Spelling has a lawyer out in the hall," Sharp said reluctantly. "He wants to talk to you."

Riles stood and set the Lysol down. He tore

off his gloves. Sharp would take care of the bottle without being told—he was a master when it came to such details.

"I don't want to talk to him," Riles said. "I will speak to the girls for a minute and then we will release them."

"Unfortunate," Sharp said. "They're our best leads."

"They will be our only suspects," Riles swore.

Alone, Riles paid the girls one last visit. They sat together in the interrogation room, on the same side of the table, not speaking. Perhaps they feared their words were being overheard. Riles wouldn't have minded eavesdropping on such a conversation, if it wasn't against the law. He sat down across from them, not bothering to turn on the tape recorder.

"I know you two were involved in the murder of Dick," he said flatly. "I'm now fairly certain you had something to do with Charlie's disappearance, too."

Hannah was sweet as ever. "That's bull."

He caught her eye. "We know more than you think we know. Charlie also bled a lot tonight, out on the road to Whistler. It's only a matter of time before we find his body."

Mary paled and put a hand to her mouth. Hannah smiled.

"Charlie is a mystery," Hannah said. "A mystery that will never be solved."

Riles did not smile. "You are a piece of work, girl. Whatever happened last night, it was planned ahead of time. But even so, you can be taken apart piece by piece. In the police business I'm what's called an owl. I never go home to sleep. I seldom stop to eat. I never stop working. I promise you, dear Hannah, I won't stop until I nail your ass to the wall."

Hannah stood. "I assume that means you can't hold us any longer."

Riles threw Mary's keys on the table. "Get out of here, both of you."

10

On the night of the murder, the night that was supposed to be reserved for fun and games, Mary stood outside, waiting in the cold snow for her boyfriend to reach her. His truck moved slowly toward her over the slippery road. Maybe he was being careful. Maybe he was trying to think what he would say to her. With all their planning, Mary had not stopped to consider what she would say to him.

Charlie pulled up beside her car, parked, and got out. He left his high beams on. Even in the harsh light and the ghastly shadows, he looked great. Just like that, even before he spoke, Mary felt her resolve crumble. She couldn't play this cruel joke on him. He didn't deserve it—he hadn't started it—and of course she still loved him. He stared at her as she processed all these thoughts and emotions. He had on the sweater she had given him for Christmas when he should have had on a heavy coat.

"I'm sorry," he said.

"I'm sorry, too," she said.

Then they were hugging and kissing.

Then all hell broke loose.

They heard a gunshot in the woods. Hannah came running out of the trees, her face a mask of horror in the truck headlights. She didn't stop running until she collided with them.

"It's Dick!" she gasped. "He's drunk! He's going to kill you, Charlie!"

Charlie stared at her as if she were the drunk one. "What is your brother doing out here?" he asked.

Hannah grabbed Mary's hands. "I ran into him down the road. He's stoned out of his mind and carrying real bullets. We have to get out of here!"

"And what are you doing here?" Charlie asked Hannah.

"Where did he get the real bullets?" Mary demanded.

"I don't think he ever had blanks," Hannah said, glancing back the way she had come. A car, also shining its high beams, was approaching rapidly. She grabbed both Mary and Charlie and dragged them toward Mary's car. "We have to get out of here!" she shouted.

"What's going on?" Charlie protested as he got in Mary's car.

"We'll explain later," Mary said, slipping in behind the wheel. Starting the car, she glanced in her rearview mirror. Dick was hanging out the driver's side, the revolver in his hand. He fired off another shot and she turned in time to see the bark on the tree in front of them splinter. Mary felt a rush of terror. There was no question he was packing live rounds. She threw the car in gear and they shot forward.

"Why is he shooting at us?" Charlie demanded.

"Because he hates you," Hannah said from the backseat, keeping her head low

"What did I do to him?" Charlie asked. "He's the one who stole my girl."

"He didn't steal me!" Mary shouted.

They heard another two shots. God knew where they went.

"Shut up and drive faster!" Hannah ordered Mary.

"I'm not running from that punk," Charlie swore.

"He has a gun, you don't," Hannah said. "You're running."

It was the wrong thing to say to Charlie.

Hannah should have known that. In response Charlie reached over and yanked the keys out of Mary's ignition. The car engine died and the car rolled forward. Mary turned to him in shock and he smiled at her.

"He won't shoot me," he said calmly. "He doesn't have the guts."

Mary swallowed. "No. Don't get out. Please?"

The car rolled to a halt and Charlie opened his door.

"I'll be back in a minute," he said. Famous last words.

Behind them they could hear Dick's car skidding to a halt. They heard his car door open and two sets of footsteps crunch through the snow. Hurrying over the flakes, like two animals—one prey, one hunter. For a moment Mary and Hannah sat as if they were made of stone, then they threw open their doors and leapt out. Suddenly there were four young people, of questionable states of mind, converging rapidly in the dark.

And it was totally dark.

No one had left car lights on.

"You sonofabitch!" Charlie said as he reached Dick. Mary could just see their outlines, just glimpse them smashing into each other. As far as she could tell, Charlie ran up to Dick and shoved him hard in the chest.

Then they both fell to the ground, wrestling in the snow.

Then a third outline leapt into the fray. Hannah.

There was shouting, screaming, cursing.

Finally Mary rushed toward them, her mind fixed on the gun.

There was another shot. Orange flame stabbed the black, and Mary saw the three of them entwined like lovers at a drunken orgy. Only now Dick was on the bottom and he no longer seemed to be moving. Indeed, there appeared to be something red and wet growing around his head. All this Mary saw in the flash of burnt powder.

Then stunned darkness. Another flash.

Mary must have blinked. This shot showed her nothing.

But she could hear Hannah screaming, screaming bloody murder as the old cliché went. Mary rushed forward, grabbed Hannah, pulled her to her feet. They hugged each other and only knew they were doing so because they were both shorter and lighter than either of the guys. Their combined breath was not ragged but torn. It was difficult to say who was more hysterical because they both must have been in shock. Mary was already trying to tell herself that nothing bad had happened. They were only in high school, it was Friday night. This was a party that had gotten a little out of hand, but everyone knew that bad things didn't happen at parties. The wet red stuff she thought she had glimpsed had been the afterglow on her retinas from the glare of the fired shot. The gun probably had blanks in it, anyway; the tree bark had splintered because it was an old tree and old trees splintered when they got old. And Charlie, her Charlie whom she loved more than anything in the whole world, would be getting up any second and telling her that she was right, everything was OK.

"Is everything OK?" Mary wept.

Hannah panted. "I don't think so."

"What do you mean you don't think so?" A long pause. "Charlie?" Mary searched the night sky and saw stars that weren't there. Red stars that threatened to swell and explode into globs of splattered blood. "Charlie?" How painful the silence was, especially after the roar of the shots. Hannah let her go.

"I'll turn on the lights in Dick's car," she said.

Mary grabbed her, held her. "No! Don't do that."

Hannah slowly unwrapped Mary's arms. "We have to see what's happened."

Mary swallowed and nodded with a head that was no longer attached to her neck. She felt as if she were floating and smothering at the same time. The sensation made her nauseous and she feared she'd be sick. But it was a tiny physical fear and could not compete with the big fear of what they would see when the lights came on. Charlie was not responding to her calls. Of course they were only in her head now, silent wails that shook to the core of her hollow being where she kept hidden horrors that she had never consciously imagined. A part of her knew she was losing her mind.

Hannah hiked through the snow toward the shadow that was Dick's car.

The headlights went on like a bomb exploding.

The guys, to Mary's surprise, were not right on top of each other. They were at least twenty feet apart. But they were both lying on their backs, and there was plenty of red stuff around both of them. Mary blinked and mentally tried to make the red stuff go away; it remained and so, finally, did the realization that Charlie was dead. No, Dick was dead as well. Yet Dick seemed but a footnote, a statistic for people who kept such records. She had never liked Dick and he had never liked her. Her own mind made her sick, that she could think that way. That she could for an instant blame Dick. She could see that his right eye was not well, that a bullet had burst through it and opened a hole into his brain. He deserved her sympathy as much as Charlie did.

Charlie looked OK, if it wasn't for the blood.

Hannah reached her and touched her. Her hand felt like ice.

"I don't know what happened," Hannah said.

"They're dead," Mary whispered.

"Shit," Hannah said. Some epithet. "What are we going to do?"

Mary looked at her, better her than Charlie. "What?"

Hannah stepped forward to Charlie, and picked a revolver out of the snow. She handed it to Mary, and Mary took it because she was afraid it might come alive, on its own accord, and start shooting again. She hardly noticed that she didn't have her gloves on. Hannah had borrowed them earlier that evening.

"We can't take the blame for this," Hannah said.

Mary struggled to breathe. It hurt. The pain in her chest was molten lava. Each time the air went through the agony, sparks flew. She couldn't understand how her heart could keep beating through such pain.

"We have to call an ambulance," she muttered. She knew she should kneel by Charlie, check his vital signs, see if he was really dead. It was just that her legs wouldn't carry her in that direction. Yet she watched as Hannah crouched by Charlie, felt for a pulse at his neck, how she briefly closed her eyes and shook her head.

"It's too late for an ambulance," Hannah said.

"Is he dead?"

Hannah sounded annoyed. "Yeah." But when she stood and looked at her brother—at his messy eye; please, could someone close it—there was no denying her grief. Her face seemed to shatter into a hundred tiny pieces. Perhaps the shock was wearing off. Hannah choked on her own voice. "Oh no. Oh God no."

They comforted each other in the night.

Then Hannah was shaking her head again, pulling away.

"We can't take the blame for this," she said again.

"But it was an accident."

Hannah laughed bitterly. "An accident? We set this up. See that gun you're holding?"

Mary realized that it was still in her hand. "Yes?"

"It's Charlie's gun. I sneaked it out of his house this afternoon when he was at the gas station."

"Why did you do that?" Mary asked, dropping it in the snow.

"Because we needed a gun for our little fun

and because the Spelling family doesn't own a gun. But I knew Charlie's father had one—he showed me how to shoot it once, with Charlie. We shot out here in fact."

"When? I didn't know that."

Hannah got loud. "It doesn't matter! What I'm saying is that this looks awful. Dick and Charlie are dead, and you and I arranged for them both to be here. I mean, our prints are on the gun."

"You didn't touch it," Mary said.

"Touch it? How do I know I didn't shoot my own brother with it? We were all rolling around in the snow. How can I prove I didn't murder them? How can you?"

"But I didn't do anything," Mary said.

"You did everything I did! You're as guilty as I am!"

Mary fought for reason. It was as if the night air refused to support it.

"But we can explain to the police," Mary said desperately. "We can tell them exactly what happened and say that no one was supposed to get hurt and that we—"

Hannah stepped toward her and grabbed her by the shoulders.

"We cannot explain that we all met here to pretend to shoot Charlie," Hannah said. "That sounds patently ridiculous."

"But it's true."

"It doesn't matter! No one will believe it. At

the same time we won't be able to convince anyone that my brother, Mr. Straight, came out here with a loaded gun to kill Charlie. He was going to be our goddamn valedictorian. Think, Mary, think hard. We're talking about the rest of our lives."

Thinking was the last thing Mary could do. Her despair was a brick on top of her skull. She gestured weakly. "What can we do then?" she whispered.

Hannah looked around, at the bodies, at the night.

"What if we make it look like they killed each other?" she said.

Mary didn't need all of her brain to know the trouble with that.

"They would both have to have been armed," she said. "There's only one gun."

Hannah put her hands to her temples. "You're right. That's a good point. OK, we don't do that. We do something else. We . . ." She stopped. "We make it look like Charlie killed Dick and then took off."

"How?"

"We get rid of Charlie's body. Put it where no one will find it. They'll think he fled in fear."

Mary shook her head. "That's crazy. The cops are smart. They'll study things, reconstruct what happened."

"Not if we move Dick's body."

"I thought you wanted to hide Charlie?" Mary said, and she couldn't believe how idiotic her words sounded to her own ears.

"We hide Charlie; we move Dick. We'll take my brother back to the Crossroads, and throw the gun into the trees there, where they'll find it. They won't be able to reconstruct what happened if they're looking in the wrong place. Besides, you're wrong, cops are all fools. You have to be a fool to want to be one in the first place. Look at Howard."

"Howard is not the one we have to worry about."

"Everyone in town knows that Charlie was mad at you for going out with Dick. If they can't find Charlie, all the heat will fall on him. They'll never suspect us. Particularly since the bullets came from Charlie's gun. The cops will probably be able to prove that."

Mary had to close her eyes for a moment. "This is all happening too fast. I don't know—I don't know what to do."

Hannah was back by her side. Opening her eyes, Mary looked into a face she hardly recognized. Hannah was forty years older and from another dimension. She was talking about things that didn't happen in the real world. Yet Dick's puddle of blood framed her head like a demonic halo. There was reality and then there was tonight.

"There is only one thing that matters now," Hannah said. "We'll never be able to explain this to anyone. They'd never believe us."

There was truth in those words.

Mary wept. "I don't want Charlie to be dead."

Hannah nodded tightly. "I hated my brother but I loved him, too. You know that. I don't want him to be dead either. But they're gone, and we can't help them now. We can only help ourselves."

Mary spoke like a child. "But what do we do with Charlie?"

"There's an old well on an abandoned farm out beyond Whistler. No one goes there. We can dump Charlie's body in there, and to the police it will be just like he ran off to Los Angeles."

Mary tried to dry her tears. "But his father—everyone—will think he was a killer."

"Mary. Everyone will think we're killers. We have no choice."

From somewhere Mary found the strength to look at Charlie, to actually study his face. He could have been sleeping, as he had slept beside her in her warm bed in the days before Christmas. Back then the two of them had been safe in their love for each other, safe from all the evil that walked outside. Of course that was the greatest lie of the entire situation. In the end, Charlie had been sleeping with his own murderer. She had said she wanted to kill him and she had. Somehow the thought gave her a perverse form of strength, the strength to move forward.

Mary nodded. "We have no choice."

They had much to do. Hannah took command. She refused to let them move the bodies until they had prepped the trunk of Mary's car with layers of plastic. To do that they had to drive to Hannah's house to get a box of plastic yard and lawn bags. There were no stores open in Maple in the middle of the night. While they were there, Hannah grabbed a bottle of Lysol, too. Mary couldn't imagine what it was for. Hannah explained that her father went to bed early. He was sound asleep and hadn't even heard her enter the house.

"One drop of blood in your car and you're in trouble," Hannah said.

"I'm in trouble?"

"Stop that, you know what I mean. We have to stick together for the next few hours. We move Dick and we dump Charlie and everything will be OK."

Mary had pain. "Quit using the word *dump*."

"Sorry."

Mary coughed. "The police will want to talk to us."

"We'll make up a story. We'll keep it simple and stupid."

Mary spoke with bitterness. "Like your plan to scare Charlie?"

"That's not fair. How did I know Dick would freak out?"

"Because he was your goddamn brother. You should have known how much he hated Charlie."

"He never talked about Charlie to me. Listen, Mary, you can't wig out on me now. I'm not spending the next twenty years in jail. Think of college, think of all the things you want to do with your life. I know you cared for Charlie, but trust me you'll love again. Tonight doesn't have to change anything."

Mary buried her head in her hands. "I can only think of Charlie's face."

They returned to the bodies. They hadn't moved. Hannah was full of energy; it was as if the Grim Reaper's favorite pill percolated in her system. She layered the trunk with plastic bags and then bagged her own brother—one going over his head and chest, the other over his legs and lower torso. She produced a roll of duct tape and sealed the bags together at his waist. Mary stood and watched her and tried to remember to breathe. Just in and out, let the air flow and life could go on.

Hannah glanced up at her as she knelt beside Dick. "Help me lift him into the trunk," she said.

Mary hesitated. "How does he feel?"

"What do you mean?"

"Does he feel like a corpse?" Mary asked.

"He feels heavy. Help me, we don't have all night."

They moved Dick back to the Crossroads and laid him in the snow. While they were gone, the blood around his eye had frozen. To Mary's immense horror, the moment they stretched him out, Hannah stood up and stepped hard on his neck. The act was sick; blood began to spurt out of his right eye. Hannah continued to jump on him. She was trying to drain him as if he were an inflatable doll she wanted to stuff in a jammed suitcase. Mary turned away and came close to vomiting.

"Don't do that," she pleaded.

"We have to make it look like he died here. We need more blood."

Mary gasped as she bent over. "I can't go through with this."

"It's too late to turn back."

They rubbed down the gun and threw it into the trees. Then they went back for Charlie. As before, Hannah bagged him and together they lifted him toward Mary's trunk. Yet they were careless. The trunk lid shot up and banged Mary in the head. She felt warm blood.

Mary was shocked at how insubstantial Charlie felt, almost like an angel made only of golden light. She wept as she held his head. She wouldn't let Hannah get near the top of him.

"Love you," she whispered.

They drove toward Whistler, Hannah behind the wheel. The abandoned farm, she said, was on their side of town, not far but very secluded. The well was deep, she assured Mary. No animals would get to Charlie. He would rest peacefully.

"Shut up," Mary muttered.

Hannah fell into a watchful silence.

The farm hardly existed anymore. There was a decrepit barn, a wooden house that looked as if it had been ravaged by a tornado. The well was made of stone, and stood alone in a barren snow-covered field like a portal into a subterranean realm of emptiness. Hannah parked beside it and jumped out, still riding on her post-killing high. Yet, even though Hannah had raised the possibility herself, Mary would have been reluctant to accuse Hannah of the deaths, at least directly. Dick had started with the gun, and Charlie reached Dick before Hannah did. The shots had been wild and unfortunate. Mary knew that much.

But what did she really know if she was able

to lift her boyfriend's body from the trunk of her car, carry it over to the rim of a stone well, and push it over the edge? True, she stopped Hannah before they committed the final atrocity. Yet the gesture lacked resolve. She reached down to tear the plastic off the top of his head. It was Hannah's turn to stop her.

"We can't spill any blood here," Hannah said.

"You said no one ever came here."

"It doesn't matter. We can leave no visible evidence."

Mary was choking. "But in time—the smell."

"No. We're standing above an underwater stream. It is another reason I chose this place. Charlie will be swept away. I promise you that he'll never be found."

"That makes me feel so much better." Mary tried to touch his head through the plastic. "I want to say goodbye to him."

"Say goodbye then."

Mary cracked then and had to turn away. "No," she moaned.

Behind her she heard a shove, a distant splash.

It was as if her heart drowned with that last sound. She felt the cold that engulfed Charlie. She saw the darkness where he drifted. And she felt that she should be floating with him, away to a world where there were no guns and no blood. Where there was only their love, worth more than any college degree, any amount of penance for sins wrongly or accidentally committed. Yet even in her despair she knew she was too weak to tell the truth, or too strong not to lie. Still, it was true, Charlie was dead and she was slowly dying.

She knew she would miss him for a long time.

11

Other acts and facts remained to be performed and told but they were mere details. They moved Charlie's truck, parking it way out of town behind a bunch of trees, on a dirt road that supposedly the loggers didn't even know existed. They soaked their hands in Lysol, drove around, and argued over their story. Then they ran into Deputy Howard, who broke the terrible news. That was how the girls met Sharp and Riles. And when the cops let them go, they escaped from the clutches of Father Spelling and his lawyer and made their way to Harvey's. There they ordered cups of black coffee and sat in a booth by the window. Ten o'clock and the place was still deserted. Maple woke up slowly Saturday mornings. Plus Harvey's was not exactly a favorite breakfast stop, more a lunch hangout.

They sat lost in their own thoughts.

Hannah smoked and Mary felt horrible.

"Well," Hannah said finally. "That wasn't so bad."

Mary snorted softly. "I can't imagine that it could have been worse."

"Not at all. They have nothing on us."

"Except they think we killed Dick and Charlie. Except for that small detail, we got off scott free."

"You're exaggerating. They were just being stupid cops. They were bluffing."

Mary counted on her fingers. "They already know Dick was killed on the road to Whistler and not at the Crossroads. That Charlie bled a huge amount in the same spot and that he is probably dead. That Charlie and Dick didn't like each other, and that you didn't like Dick, and that I was mad at both Dick and Charlie. That we were at very incriminating locations with our walking and running shoes on. I mean, in a few hours they learned all that. If they're just stupid cops then I'd hate to see the real thing. What will they know in a week? Where you bought the Lysol?"

Hannah frowned. "I should have got rid of that."

"Why didn't you?"

Hannah picked up a tiny plastic packet of

catsup from a table container. She squeezed it, slowly making it burst in her left hand. The red juice, as it squished onto the Formica tabletop, looked nauseating. Mary wished she'd play with the sugar instead.

"There wasn't time," Hannah said. "We ran into Deputy Howard right after drenching our hands, remember?"

"You screwed up."

"I screwed up? What about you, Miss Guilty Looking? Every time they pressed you to spill your guts, you cringed. I told you just to act cool."

"How could I act cool? Your brother is dead and my boyfriend is missing. If I'd acted cool I would have come off sounding like you."

"What is that supposed to mean?" Hannah asked.

"Dick is dead. You should have broken down in front of them and wept."

"I broke down and wept when they had me alone."

"Yeah, you shed a few tears and then conveniently put them away. That made you seem even more guilty."

"I did a hell of a lot better than you. Your answer for everything was, "I can't remember, officers." Christ, it was as if you were suddenly suffering from amnesia."

"I didn't want to complicate our lies," Mary said.

"You just made them sound like lies."

"They grilled me far more than you. I held up pretty well, I thought. I never deviated from the basic story. Which is another thing that I think was a big mistake. Why did we have to say we saw Charlie at all? A dozen witnesses will confirm that he was never at the Pizza Palace."

"That's bullshit. The waiters at that joint can't count, never mind remember who they served. We had to establish that we'd seen Charlie, that everything was cool, and that was all you knew."

Mary lowered her voice. "What if they find his body?"

"Impossible. We've been over this. It has washed under the earth."

Mary grimaced. "I can't believe we dumped him like that."

Hannah put out her cigarette and wiped the catsup off her hand with a napkin. She reached out and took Mary's hand. "You can grieve, Mary. That's natural. But you must be strong. You can't let yourself suffer pangs of guilt in public. People will read into them. You know we planned none of this, not really. It happened because Dick had to go and get loaded and lose his mind."

Mary stared at Hannah's hand, how she held her fingers with hers.

With affection. Almost as if they were lovers.

"You said he was fine," Mary muttered. "When and where did he get the drugs?"

Hannah sighed. "I don't know. One thing for sure, I don't think he went to the movies after he said goodbye to us at the Pizza Palace."

"When and where did you see him last?"

Hannah shrugged. "Just off the town square, not long before I saw you again. Why?"

"Because his state of mind changed radically in the time he was out of our sight."

"You're telling me. But it must be what the cops said. He took some PCP."

"Dick was never a hard drug user," Mary said.

Hannah took her hand back and studied her friend. "What are you getting at?"

"That there are some huge unanswered questions here."

"Yeah. But why are you asking me?"

Mary was annoyed. "My boyfriend died last night, I need to ask you these questions. I deserve answers. Who else am I going to ask?"

"Lower your voice."

Mary snapped. "No one is listening."

"You don't know that." Hannah glanced at the counter, at a pimply kid munching on a jelly doughnut. "For the next few months, the walls have ears."

Mary spoke quietly. "You're not answering my questions."

"I told you, I didn't know anything about Dick's drug habits. There was a lot he kept private."

"How come you didn't check to make sure he was carrying blanks?"

"That was stupid, I should have. But in a way it doesn't matter. If he intended to kill Charlie, it would have only taken him a moment to switch to live rounds."

"But why would he want to kill Charlie?" Mary asked.

"Because of you."

"That's bullshit. Dick wanted to screw me, he didn't want to marry me. He wouldn't have thrown his whole life away over inconsequential Mary Dammon."

"Dick was stoned last night. He needed no more motivation than that."

"Where were you before you ran into the clearing and started shouting at Charlie and me?"

"You know, where you dropped me off."

"That's impossible. You knew what Dick was up to, even when his car was still up the road from us. You had to have seen him before he reached the Crossroads to know his state of mind."

158

Hannah paused. "I did see him. I saw that he was stoned."

Mary sat back. "So he stopped before he reached the Crossroads and spoke to you?"

Hannah paused. "Yeah."

"What did you talk about?"

"Nothing. He was too loaded, too fired up to get Charlie."

"But he had a car, you didn't. How did you outrun him to the Crossroads?"

"I ran as fast as I could when I saw what he was up to. I even tried to take his gun from him."

"Really?"

"Yeah. I don't understand you. You were there, you saw what happened. This was all a screw-up. I didn't have anything to do with who got shot."

Mary considered. "It was dark when they got shot. Very dark as you'll recall. I didn't see anything."

Hannah fished for her pack of cigarettes in her pants. "You sound like you don't believe me."

"I didn't say that."

"You implied it, and that's a big mistake with me."

"Really?" Mary paused, thinking. "How many times did Dick . . ." She stopped herself, something stopped her. Hannah came alive.

"How many times did Dick what?"

"Nothing."

"What were you going to ask?" Hannah persisted.

"Nothing. What were you saying?"

"You know. Right now, in the whole world, I am the only real friend you have."

Mary was miserably amused. "Because we're partners in crime?"

Hannah flicked her lighter. "In a sense. I keep telling you that we have to depend on each other now. If one cracks, we both go down." Hannah blew smoke and reached for Mary's hand again. She tried to catch Mary's eye. Her nails brushed Mary's skin as she added, "I need you, Mary. You need me."

Mary held her eye. "You like that, don't you? This dependency?"

Hannah stiffened. "I have never made a pass at you."

"I think you're making one now."

Various emotions played across Hannah's face. But they were too jumbled to decipher easily. Hannah leaned closer, till her face was only inches away. Smoke swam between them and irritated Mary's eyes. Hannah's pretty hazel eyes seemed to grow moist as well. Certainly, she spoke in a gentler tone than Mary had ever heard her use before.

"Would that be so bad?" she asked.

Mary was not given a chance to reply.

It was right then that she saw Charlie.

He was staggering down the center of the street, coming from the direction of Whistler. He looked like a shivering drunk who had spent the night in the woods. His clothes were obviously wet, covered with mud instead of blood. He still had on the sweater Mary had made him for Christmas, even though it was now torn in six places. But from the expression on his face, even at a distance of two hundred yards, he looked like he might not recognize Mary. Literally, he was moving like a zombie, somebody freshly returned from the dead. Seeing him Mary didn't immediately feel the wave of relief she should have. He looked so weird that she thought the horror of the last twelve hours had just taken a supernatural twist. He was so white that she could feel her own blood draining from her face as she stared at him.

Hannah turned to see what Mary was gaping at and almost inhaled her cigarette.

"Oh no," she moaned.

"It can't be," Mary whispered.

"He's alive," Hannah gasped.

Mary wept. "Are we sure it's Charlie?"

"Of course it is," Hannah said.

Mary panted. "But he was dead. You said he was dead."

"I thought he was dead." Hannah got up.

"Come on, we'd better get to him before the rest of the town does."

They hurried out of Harvey's, leaving their coffee half finished. They caught up to him as he staggered into a telephone pole with his face and then plopped down on the sidewalk on his ass. He had been leaning toward the side of the road since they spotted him. His eyes were open but he wasn't seeing anything. Mary knelt by his side while Hannah remained standing.

"Charlie!" Mary cried. "Are you OK?"

He stared at her strangely. "Mary," he mumbled.

Then he collapsed unconscious in her arms.

Mary hugged him tightly. She must have been crying, there were slippery wet spots on her face. "Oh, Charlie, what have we done to you?" she whispered as she ran her hand through his hair. He was soaked, and cold as ice. There was some blood on his clothes, but it looked as if the sweater had been put through a washing machine before the blood had a chance to dry. She thought of the underwater stream Hannah had mentioned. Unknown to Hannah, it must have come out somewhere on the surface of the earth. Of course there was the question of the bullet Charlie took. He didn't seem to have any holes in him but she'd need to examine him more closely. Hannah spoke behind her. She didn't sound happy.

Mary's own happiness was an emotion she had yet to allow. But it was coming, she could feel it coming. A wave of clear joy, strong enough to wash away all the trash that had gone down.

"Give me your keys, I'll get your car," Hannah said. "We have to get him out of sight."

Mary handed over her keys.

She stared at Hannah as her friend went for the car.

Somehow Mary knew what was coming next.

Hannah returned shortly and they loaded Charlie into the backseat. He was snoring loudly and breathing easily, although still shivering. Mary climbed in beside him and felt his chest in the area where he had supposedly bled to death. Up front Hannah steered the car out of town.

"Turn the heat on full blast," Mary said as she pulled off her jacket. "I think he's suffering from hypothermia."

"He should be suffering from more than that," Hannah muttered.

Mary understood. Yet, the more she examined him, the more confused she was. Finally she raised his sweater and shirt, past his nipples. Then she almost burst out laughing.

She hadn't known Charlie was Catholic.

He had on a Saint Christopher's medal. A *badly* mangled one.

It looked like it had taken a .38 slug.

The skin had burst beneath the medal. Charlie would need stitches, and he had obviously bled a great deal from the chest wound. Yet the medal had absorbed the brunt of the impact of the bullet and saved his life. Mary did laugh a little as she pulled his shirt back down.

"He's going to be OK," Mary said. "But we've got to get him to a hospital."

"We're not going to the hospital," Hannah said flatly. "Climb over the seat, get up here. We have to talk."

Mary did as she was told. The heat was flooding the car and she knew it would not be long before Charlie stopped shivering. He might even wake up soon, and start talking. Mary knew Hannah was terrified of what he might say.

"Where are we going?" Mary asked.

"Out of town."

Mary took a deep breath of the warm air. "I see."

Hannah whirled. "Do you see, Mary? The whole picture?"

Mary stared straight ahead. "Yes."

"Do you want to talk about it?"

Mary shrugged. "What's there to talk about?"

"We have no choice."

"Your favorite line."

Hannah pounded the steering wheel. "What do you want to do? Go back to the police and tell them everything we said was a lie? We do that and we go to jail for a long time. Because after so many lies, they'll never believe that we didn't purposely kill my brother."

"I hear you."

"Then why don't you say something!"

Mary spoke bitterly. "What do you want me to say? That Charlie has to die? You want the words to come out of my mouth? So that later you can say it was my idea?"

Hannah reached over and touched her shoulder. Her next question caught Mary by surprise. Yet it shouldn't have—it was the question of the hour really, the one upon which everything that had previously happened turned. It was the seed of the night's insanity, Mary realized, and the fun that was still to come.

"Do you know how I feel about you?" Hannah asked.

Mary sighed. "Yeah, I know."

Hannah sounded scared, finally. So exposed.

"How do you feel about me?" she asked.

Mary spoke carefully. "You're my friend."

"Your good friend?"

"Yeah. My good friend."

Hannah took that in, it seemed she did.

"I don't want to do this. I really don't."

"I know," Mary said quietly.

Hannah hesitated. "Are you with me?"

Mary thought of first grade. Learning to count.

From day one, she knew how to count all the way to ten.

"Yes," Mary said.

"Are you sure?"

"Yes."

"It can be like it was. No one saw him."

"I know," Mary said.

"It can be painless. He doesn't have to suffer."

Mary closed her eyes. Behind her Charlie probably dreamed.

"That's all that matters," she whispered.

Hannah squeezed her shoulder. "You won't regret it."

They returned to the deserted farm. Mary was surprised, the place hadn't worked the first time around. Hannah explained that they could still use it as a temporary holding place. Sort of like a temporary grave, Mary thought.

Yet before they drove to the farm, they stopped at Charlie's truck, stashed deep in the woods. Hannah said she wanted to check it out, make sure it hadn't been found. She explained that they would move it later as well, when things cooled off. As if the minds of the detectives would change with the weather. While Mary waited in her car with sleeping Charlie, Hannah went inside Charlie's truck.

Mary thought that odd. Yet, not really.

One. Two. Three. Four. Five . . .

At the farm Hannah stopped the car near the barn. As she started to get out she said that they had to get Charlie into the barn. Of course he'd wake when they lifted him so what Hannah really meant was that they had to kill Charlie before they stashed his dead body in the barn. With Hannah the things that weren't spoken were the most revealing. Mary grabbed her arm as she started to get out.

"I want to do it," Mary said.

Hannah paused. "Can you?"

"I don't want you to do it."

Hannah understood. "He's unconscious. You can use anything, a large rock or something."

Mary opened her door. "Something."

Charlie must have been suffering from blood loss as well as the cold. Actually, he was probably still recovering from floating under the ground for God knew how long. He did not wake as they lifted him out of the backseat and put him on his back in the snow. Staring down at him, Mary couldn't believe that they had the nerve to treat any human being this way. The perverse irony of it was that Hannah was standing on the other side of him waiting for Mary to whack him.

"How do you want to do it?" Hannah asked.

Mary looked around. "A brick maybe. Do you see any?"

Hannah searched, then pointed. "There's one there on top of that pile of junk under that white pine."

"Let's get it," Mary said, stepping around Charlie to join Hannah. Together they walked toward the discarded brick. They paused in front of the pile with the brick, and the moment was crucial. For Mary paused longer, and so it was Hannah who bent over to pick it up.

As she did so Mary slipped behind her and shoved her forward.

Hannah's face smashed into the brick, her rear up in the air. Mary yanked up the back of Hannah's jacket to reveal the revolver tucked in her belt. Mary grabbed the gun and pulled it loose. She moved quickly and precisely, without fear. She had positioned herself perfectly to take aim between her friend's eyes before Hannah could recover her balance. Hannah now stood crouched like a wary animal.

"How did you know?" Hannah whispered.

"Riles said that four shots had been fired from the gun they found. I remembered that there had been six shots. That meant there must have been another gun."

"When did you remember?"

"When I saw Charlie alive." Mary waved the revolver. "Get in the barn."

Hannah trembled. "You won't kill me. I know you, Mary, you're not a killer."

Mary cocked the hammer. "You do not know me, Hannah."

Hannah raised her arms and walked in the direction of the barn. Mary followed closely but not so close that Hannah could whirl around and disarm her. Mary had seen enough thrillers to know about that little trick. Hannah seemed to move in slow motion agony. Her trembling had changed to outright shaking, and she was weeping softly. She risked a glance over her shoulder.

"Please don't shoot me," she whispered.

"Shut up. Keep walking."

Hannah choked. "I don't want to die."

"Charlie doesn't want to die either. Dick didn't want to die."

Hannah was a mass of nerves. "I'm sorry, Mary. Please believe me. I didn't want it to happen this way."

"Bullshit. You set this up from the beginning. Looking back, it's all so obvious. Charlie found out about Dick kissing me at the Sadie Hawkins' because you phoned and told him. You manipulated me into wanting revenge and then you manipulated your brother into playing the fool in your scheme. You drugged him with the PCP right after you left me at the Pizza Palace. You wanted his brain boiling. You put the live ammo in Charlie's gun, and you told Dick just to shoot close to us, not at us. Even stoned, he listened to you. Why shouldn't he listen to his own sister? He probably thought it would make the evening more exciting. Then you manipulated Charlie into stopping the car and getting out to face Dick. You knew Charlie well—that he would never run from your brother. Finally you seemingly randomly jumped into the fray to accomplish your own hidden agenda. From the outside, in the pitch black, you looked brave. You were risking your life to save two angry young guys from hurting each other. The only thing about your hidden agenda was that it included a hidden gun. You shot them both with the gun I'm holding. A gun you later stashed in Charlie's truck. You did it right in front of me and I didn't even see it. Tell me, Hannah, how were you able to shoot so well in the dark? Are you a vampire or are you just lucky?"

Hannah had stopped and dropped her arms. She panted hard. On her face lines of terror. "If I tell you the truth will you let me go?" she asked meekly.

Mary's gun hand shook. "Damn you! You tell me or I shoot you right now where you stand!"

Hannah moaned. "I bought some of those special night glasses at an army surplus store in Portland. They were old and cracked and expensive but they worked. They let me see in the dark. I just wore them for a second. Then I put them back in my coat pocket."

"Where are they now?" Mary demanded.

"In Charlie's truck."

Mary smiled thinly and glanced back at Charlie, who continued to sleep peacefully. She had to get him out of the elements soon. "You had everything figured perfectly. Too bad you didn't count on Charlie's St. Christopher medal, and the fact that this old well's underground stream leads out to fresh air somewhere. You're smart Hannah, but it's Charlie who's lucky." Mary paused and took a step closer. She was so pissed she actually rammed the barrel against Hannah's throat. "The only trouble is I don't know what all these revelations make me."

Hannah gasped. "You can't kill me. I can't die."

Mary chuckled. "Wrong, girl. You can die. You deserve to die. Hearing you talk like that makes me feel better about killing you. Keep walking, get into the barn, I don't want to mess up this nice clean snow."

Hannah bawled. "You can't do this to me!"

Mary smacked her in the face with the gun. "Stop it! You started all this and you're going to finish it. You have nothing to complain about. You'll play Charlie's part—the murderer who fled the scene of the crime. Then when things cool down, I'll come out here and move you to a better hiding place. Until then you'll be a good little dead body and lie out here in this barn and try not to rot too much."

Hannah entered the realm of shock. She couldn't speak. Mary had to threaten to smack her again to get her to move. Hannah staggered toward the nearby barn as if she had already been shot. Mary wondered what it would be like to pull the trigger, to watch her friend die. She longed for the darkness that had hidden Dick's death. Just a flash of fire, then a glimpse of the nightmare. Mary knew that this moment would haunt her.

The interior of the barn was nothing. Four ugly wooden walls. A place to hide despicable acts. Mary gestured for Hannah to move toward the corner. At the last moment Hannah dropped down on her knees in front of Mary. She placed her hands together near her heart in an attitude of prayer. Her pretty hazel eyes were murky swamp gas now. She stared up at Mary with the anguish of a tortured child.

"I thought you loved me," Hannah whispered.

Mary bit her lip, trying to keep her right arm steady.

"No," she said tightly. "I don't love you."

Hannah nodded as if in acceptance. "Please don't hurt my face. My father never loved me either, but he always told me how pretty I was."

Mary nodded. "Goodbye, Hannah."

Hannah closed her eyes. "Bye."

Mary shot her in the heart. Hannah fell forward on her face. Mary rolled her over before she left the barn. She had to see her friend's face one last time, perhaps to understand for the remainder of her life exactly what she had done. Hannah's chest was stained red. But her face, the face of the monster who had had the nerve to wipe two innocent people out of existence, looked like that of a pretty young girl taking a nap. Had her father been there, he might have felt the desire to wipe away the lock of blond hair that had fallen on her face. Mary brushed it aside.

The guilty were never executed.

The moment of death brought an instant of innocence.

Mary turned and walked out of the barn.

Outside she wiped off the gun and threw it in some bushes.

12

Lieutenant Riles and Lieutenant Sharp were contemplating going home and going to bed. Neither had a family, no one waiting for them. The idea of sleep was becoming more inviting with each passing hour. The tech guys were out at the scene of the murder, Kohner was still dissecting Dick, and Mary and Hannah were probably shopping for clothes for their next high school dance. Of course Riles had doubts about the latter. He suspected the girls were up to much more dangerous activities.

"We're not doing much good here," Sharp said as the two of them worked on yet another cup of coffee. "Should we go back out to the Crossroads?"

Riles shook his head. "We'd just get in the way."

"Maybe we should check in with Kohner again."

"If he finds something he'll let us know."

"Then what are we doing here?" Sharp asked.

"We're supposed to be thinking."

"My brains stopped working when the girls left." Sharp yawned. "Are you having any profound thoughts?"

"Linda Hoppe is on my mind."

Sharp was surprised. "We are getting desperate, aren't we?"

"Perhaps not. All these girls grew up together. They know stuff about each other that could take us months to discover without them."

"But Linda? She has less working brain tissue than Dick's."

"Her stupidity could be her biggest asset. She doesn't know when to keep her mouth shut." Riles stood. "I'd like to talk to her again."

Sharp also got up slowly. "About what?"

"I keep thinking how the tire tracks led away from the second group of blood puddles that we found. I'd give a lot to know where those tracks ended up." Riles paused as he headed for the door. "You don't have to come. You can rest if you want."

"I told you, I go where you go." Sharp had to laugh. "Even to Linda Hoppe's house."

As it turned out, Linda was not at home, but at the Day Glow Donut. The detectives found her eating a chocolate-covered doughnut and drinking milk with friends. The latter cleared out as soon as they saw the lieutenants. Linda told them to get lost, in fact; she said it with authority, letting them know she was important and that she knew things they didn't. Even though their previous meeting had not ended well, Linda looked positively ecstatic to see them. She even offered them one of her doughnuts. The police respectfully declined. Linda rubbed her hands together excitedly.

"Have you caught them yet?" she asked.

"Who?" Sharp asked.

"The murderers, of course."

"But we thought you thought Mary did it?" Riles asked.

Linda waved her hand. "I've thought about it more and changed my mind. It's too obvious that Mary is the killer. I mean, like, she announced to practically the whole world that she wanted to kill Charlie. Why would she do that and then go ahead and do it? I mean, shit, it doesn't make sense."

"Linda," Sharp said patiently. "It is Dick who's dead."

"I know, I know. But these things can happen in pairs, and Hannah and Dick are twins. We talked about that. I think there's a connection."

Riles and Sharp had to exchange a look on that one.

"We fail to see it," Sharp said.

Linda brushed her dark hair aside—it was no longer pinned up with Excalibur—and leaned forward. "I think it was Hannah who killed Dick. She shot him so she'd inherit all her dad's money. It's perfect motivation."

"But you said last time that Hannah and Dick loved each other," Sharp said.

Linda was unmoved. "What is love when we're talking about millions of dollars? I mean, you guys know what makes the world go round. It sure ain't love, come on. It's cash and sex—that's it, nothing else matters. And if you don't have one, you can't get the other."

"Linda," Riles said, "you have known Mary and Hannah all your life, right?"

Linda sat back, seemingly hurt that they weren't interested in her theories.

"Yeah," she said carefully. "But I wouldn't help them kill someone, if that's what you're saying."

"I'm not implying that you would," Riles said politely. "I was just wondering if, as you girls grew up together, you had any favorite hiding places out of town that you'd go? Say, when you were eight to twelve. Places you used to ride to on your bikes?"

Linda made a face. "What a weird question.

I mean, we all had bikes and liked to ride everywhere. Hannah didn't kill her brother because he had a bike and she didn't. She had one, too. It was a green Schwinn mountain bike, totally radical."

Riles smiled. "I know you're right about that. But if you could humor me for a moment, where did you girls like to go when you wanted to get away from everything?"

Linda suddenly clapped her hands together. "I know what you're asking! You want to know where they might have dumped Charlie's body!"

Riles nodded. "That's it exactly."

Linda thought real hard. "Hannah and me used to go to this deserted farm sometimes. It's not that far from here, a few miles out on the road to Whistler."

Both cops sat up straight.

"Can you give us exact directions?" Riles asked.

"Sure." And Linda did give them directions, several versions of them. After about ten minutes and many questions they basically knew how to get to the farm. When she was done Linda wanted to know if they thought she'd be interviewed on TV.

"Probably," Riles said. "You're obviously important to this case."

Linda smiled. "Cool." Then she stopped

smiling. "Oh, I forgot to tell you guys something. It's real important, I don't know how I could have forgot."

"What?" Sharp asked.

"I thought I saw Charlie."

"*What?*" they both said.

Linda was unsure. "I couldn't swear it was him, but it sure looked like him."

"When and where do you think you saw him?" Riles asked quietly.

Linda shrugged. "This morning, wandering down the middle of the street. I didn't get a good look at him. It might have been somebody else."

"Didn't you stop to make sure who it was?" Sharp asked.

Linda took a bite of her doughnut. "No. I was too busy."

"What were you doing?" Riles asked.

Linda chewed. "Stuff."

In the snow at the deserted farm that Linda said was a favorite childhood haunt of Hannah's, they found fresh tire tracks in the snow. Two sets actually, both from the same car. Sharp and Riles studied them carefully, crouched together a few feet from a stone well.

"These look like the treads on Mary's tires," Riles said. "The same tires near the two puddles of blood."

"Are you sure?" Sharp asked.

"Pretty damn sure."

Sharp glanced at the well. "Do you think they dumped Charlie in there?"

"I think that's more likely than the possibility that Charlie was walking around town this morning."

They stood and walked over to the well and peered down into it. The well seemed to swallow the faint sound of their breathing, a tunnel into perpetual night. Far below, maybe fifty feet, they could hear running water.

"If they threw him in here he's gone," Sharp said.

"I'm not so sure about that. I've been out here before. I think the underground stream comes out somewhere."

"Where?"

Riles frowned. "I can't remember."

"You've been spending too much time with Linda Hoppe."

"I believe it. Let's check out the barn."

The barn was empty.

Except for footprints in the dust, and some red stuff in the corner. Excited, they hurried toward the latter but their excitement faded when Riles touched one drop of it and rolled it slowly between his fingers. He sniffed the red gook.

"Catsup," he said.

Sharp was deflated. "Damn."

Riles studied a nearby set of footprints. "Mary's New Balance running shoes." He pointed deeper into the corner. "Hannah's Nike walking shoes."

"Tell me, how can you tell what's a walking shoe and what's a running shoe?"

"Experience." Riles added, "I sold sports shoes to put myself through college."

"I didn't know that."

"It was only a part time job," Riles said.

"No. I didn't know you went to college. I'll have to treat you with more respect." Sharp nodded to the catsup on Riles's fingers. "If only that belonged to Charlie, we'd have a stronger case against the girls."

Riles stared at the red stuff. "But it fooled you for a second, didn't it?"

"Yeah. Didn't it fool you?"

"Yes. For a moment." Riles studied the prints some more. "I wonder if it fooled someone else."

"What do you mean?"

"Why is there catsup here?" Riles asked. "I think that's the important question."

Sharp was doubtful. "You might be reading too much into it. Somebody probably just sat here and ate fries."

"No. This catsup is fresh. In fact, in this cold, it should be frozen and it's not."

"I'm not following you," Sharp admitted.

"Catsup is one of the few substances people

have on hand that can look like blood. I wonder if one of the girls used it on the other girl to fake her out. Or rather, I wonder if one of the girls used it on *herself* to fake the other out."

Sharp nodded. "To fake the fact that she was bleeding."

"Exactly."

"It sounds like you're reaching again."

Riles stood. "I want to go see the girls again. Now."

Sharp got up. "We have no right to question them so soon after their release."

Riles felt another chill, that came, not from outside but from inside himself.

He kept thinking how cold Hannah was. How smart.

"We'll tell them it's a social call," Riles said, turning for the barn door.

Sharp followed. "Whose house should we visit first?"

"Were Mary's parents home when we released her?"

"I understood they had a few hours left to drive before they reached Maple."

"Then we go to Mary's," Riles said.

13

in his chest.

At Mary Dammon's house, in her bedroom where she first made love to Charles Gallagher, Mary sat on her bed beside Charlie. He was naked and asleep under the covers. She'd had trouble getting him inside the house and then even more trouble getting his clothes off. It was only now, finally, after running a portable electric heater on him for an hour, that he began to feel warm. She had already bandaged his chest wound. Gently she brushed his hair as she gazed at his handsome face. She wished that he would wake up soon so that she could tell him how much she loved him.

"I do, you know," she whispered. "Even though I almost got you killed."

Charlie opened his eyes and stared at the ceiling.

"Did you say something?" he croaked.

"Oh, Charlie!" she cried, burying her face in his chest.

He groaned. "That hurts."

She remembered his injury. "Sorry. How are you feeling?"

He was sleepy. "Good. Where am I?"

"My bedroom. You're safe now."

"From what?"

She took his hand and leaned close. "Do you remember what happened last night?"

He thought for a moment. "No."

"What is the last thing you remember?"

"We were at the Crossroads. You were there. You said you were sorry."

She smiled through her tears. "You said you were sorry, too. Do you remember?"

He yawned. "Yes."

"Did you mean it?"

"Yes." He yawned loudly. "I love you, Mary."

Then his eyes closed. He was snoring again.

She kissed him on the forehead. "I love you more than I realized, Charlie."

Mary stood and quietly left the bedroom.

Hannah was sitting in Mary's living room in fresh warm clothes. She lifted her hand and there was a revolver in it. The one Mary had thrown into the bushes after killing Hannah.

"Oh," Mary said, freezing.

Hannah waved the gun. "Sit down."

Mary sat in a chair across from her. She was beyond shock.

"How?" Mary gasped.

Hannah did not smile. "Blanks. In Harvey's, just before Charlie turned up, you let it slip that you knew how many shots Dick had fired. I knew then that you knew I was the killer. I knew you'd go for my gun when you had the chance. When we stopped at Charlie's truck, before we went back out to the farm, I loaded it with blanks. I had bought the blanks before, to show Dick." She cocked the hammer. "But I have live rounds with me now in case you're wondering."

Mary swallowed. "I was not wondering."

Hannah glanced around. "When do your parents get home?"

"Soon."

"How soon?"

"I don't know."

Hannah considered. "It doesn't matter. We won't be here long. What are you looking at?"

"A ghost. Why the big emotional display at the farm?"

Hannah was reflective. "To see if you could be moved." She held her eye. "To see if you cared."

"Why should I care about a murderer?"

Hannah drew in a ragged breath. "You shot me, Mary. How could you do that to me?"

"I enjoyed it. Give me the gun and I'll shoot you again."

Hannah's expression darkened. "I'm going to kill you, both of you. You must know."

"Then I'll be the one who fled the scene because of her guilt?"

"Yes. I have it all planned. When you vanish, the cops will stop hassling me."

"I'm not going anywhere. You're going to have to shoot me here. And I'm sure I'll bleed a lot. I'll make a point of it before I die. My parents really are on their way home. You won't be able to clean up the mess before they arrive. No one, especially the cops, will think I left town because of guilt." Mary paused. "So you see you don't have it all planned after all."

Hannah sat up. "I can make you move."

Mary shook her head. "Nope. Even if you threaten to shoot Charlie, I won't budge from this chair. Go ahead he's in the bedroom. Put the gun to his head and threaten me. Better yet put the barrel of your gun in my mouth like they do on TV and try to scare me big time."

Hannah was bitter. "I only wanted your love. Was that too much to ask?"

"Yeah. You're gay and I'm not. Killing your brother didn't change that. Also, before you get started, don't try pulling that poor lonely homosexual routine on me. You did not murder your brother because you're gay. I know lots of wonderful well-balanced lesbians. You killed him because you're a loon. It's as simple as that."

Hannah had tears. "And why did you try to kill me?"

"Stupid question. You deserved it."

Hannah stood and pointed the revolver down at her. "I pull this trigger and a bullet goes in your heart. Like that, you no longer exist on this planet. You know I'm fully capable of doing it. I'm not bluffing."

Mary sighed, and she was terribly afraid.

But she knew she couldn't show the fear.

"Even if you put a bullet in my heart, it won't make room in there for you," Mary said.

Hannah was having trouble breathing. "What will make room?"

"Go to the police. Take the blame for what happened. Then talk your dad into getting me into Stanford." Mary paused. "Then maybe I'll love you."

"Now is not the time to mock me."

Mary softened. "I know."

Hannah spread her hands. "What can I do? I can't go to jail. For Christsakes I hate having to hang out in my own bedroom. I have to kill you both."

"No. Put the gun down, leave town. I won't tell the cops the real story."

"But they'll hunt me down."

"But they won't find you," Mary said. "Not you."

Hannah shook her dangerous head. "You'll talk. Eventually you'll talk."

"I promise I won't."

Hannah shouted. "God! How can you expect me to trust you when you tried to kill me an hour ago?"

The front doorbell rang. Hannah whirled. "Don't answer it!" she gasped.

Mary was able to peer out the window from where she sat.

"It's the detectives," she said. "They must have heard your voice. I have to answer it or they'll get suspicious."

"No," Hannah snapped.

Mary stood. "We have no choice." She stepped toward the door. Hannah grabbed her by the hair and rammed the barrel of the revolver into her neck. She was stronger than Mary would have imagined.

"Say the wrong thing and I shoot them both and then you. Understand?"

Mary nodded. "I'll be cool."

Hannah released her. "Get them to leave quickly."

Mary answered the door. Sharp and Riles didn't look as if they'd gone to bed yet. Mary could relate, and then some. She forced a bright smile.

"Why Lieutenant Sharp and Lieutenant Riles. What a pleasant surprise." She opened the storm door. "Please come in."

The detectives entered the house and looked around.

Hannah was back in her chair, her revolver and gun hand concealed under a *People* magazine.

"Hi, officers," Hannah said sweetly.

"Hello," Sharp said.

"Are your parents home yet?" Riles asked Mary.

"No. In a couple of hours." She gestured to the sofa beside her vacated chair. "Would you like some coffee? I have a fresh pot in the kitchen."

"Yes, please," Sharp said.

Mary turned to Riles. "Does he speak for you?"

Riles nodded, clearly suspicious. "We take it black."

Mary disappeared into the kitchen. She thought of disappearing out the back door. But she didn't want to leave the cops with crazy Hannah, and Charlie was still asleep in the bedroom. Fortunately she really did have a pot of coffee brewed. She poured four cups, one for each of them, and returned to the living room with a tray. Hannah was charming the police; they must have wondered at the improvement in her disposition. Riles in particular seemed alert to danger. He never picked up his coffee cup, but kept his hands close to his coat, to his weapon.

"What have you girls been up to since we saw you last?" he asked.

They both forced grins. For different reasons.

"Nothing," Hannah said.

"Just plotting to assassinate the president," Mary said.

Hannah giggled. "Mary! Don't tell them anything they don't need to know."

Mary also chuckled. "But I want them to know that we're not as sweet as we look."

At her last comment Riles moved his hand closer to his coat. There was no doubt that he was studying Hannah closely. She was not wearing the *People* magazine over her hand very well. Hannah sensed his scrutiny and began to fidget.

"What do you guys want?" she asked finally.

"Since we saw you last we've been out to an old deserted farm," Riles said. "It's out toward Whistler. The place is terribly run down with a stone well out front. Do you girls know the place?"

Mary nodded. "I know it."

Hannah hesitated. "I'm not sure I've been there. Why did you two go out there?"

192

Riles acted casual. "We were looking for Charlie."

A shadow crossed Hannah's face.

Mary prayed Riles understood what that meant.

Hannah took a deep breath. "I see. Did you find him?"

Riles was tense. "No. But we found some interesting things."

Hannah's eyes narrowed. "Oh? What?"

The detective was not given an opportunity to explain.

Charlie walked into the room right then.

He sat down in the remaining living room chair. He had a sheet wrapped around him and nothing else on. Mary still thought he looked cute, even with the huge white bandage on his bare chest. He glanced around at everyone as if he was only half awake. Then he blinked in Hannah's direction and his vision cleared. He lifted his arm and pointed.

"Hey," he said. "I just remembered. She shot me."

Riles went for his gun. Hannah was quicker. Riles froze, catching Hannah's eye, and slowly brought down his hand. Hannah stood and covered the four of them with the revolver. Charlie blinked again but now he was showing no sign of falling back asleep.

"Wow," Charlie said.

"No one move," Hannah snapped.

"I'd do what she says," Mary said carefully.

Riles stared at Hannah as he spoke. "You have a gun but you have nowhere to go. There's no point in making the situation worse than it is. Now I am going to slowly stand and put out my hand and you're going to slowly give me the gun. OK?"

Hannah shook her head tightly. "Move an inch and I'll shoot."

Sharp glanced at his partner and shook his head slightly. Yet Riles had eyes for Hannah only. He was the hero type, Mary thought. He might be a dead hero in a couple of minutes. Any of them could die in that span of time, even her beloved Charlie.

Mary knew what she had to do next but she was afraid. Her false bravado of a few minutes ago was gone. She couldn't stop thinking what it would be like to take a bullet in the gut. How her intestines would explode with gross matter, how the blood would gush out and soak her parents' carpet. Her mother and father might come home to find her that way. Their beloved daughter, their dead daughter.

Yet Mary knew she had to pay for what she'd done in the last twelve hours. Pay, big time, to God, for bringing Charlie back from beneath the earth. She knew she owed these officers as well for risking their lives to discover the truth. They were brave men, both of them, and she couldn't let them be victims of this madness that she had indirectly started. She watched as Riles ignored Hannah's warning and started to stand.

"No," Mary said firmly. "Let me."

Riles looked at her. "No."

Mary stood. "Let me."

Riles hesitated then nodded.

Hannah turned the gun on her. "Stay."

Mary took a step forward. "Dick is dead. Charlie almost died. You pretended to be dead. I guess it's my turn now, Hannah. What's it going to be for me?"

Hannah was a nervous breakdown happening in a five-second span.

Hannah shook her head frantically. "Don't make me do it."

Mary's eyes moistened. She could feel how close death was.

"I don't want to die," Mary said. "I want to go to college. I want to love Charlie. I want to do all kinds of stuff. I know you want to do that stuff, too, and that you wanted to do some of it with me."

Hannah was in pain. The gun shook.

"But that's impossible now, isn't it?" Hannah asked.

Mary nodded and took another step. "Yeah. Everything got messed up. But Lieutenant Riles is right, if you shoot any of us it won't help. Everything will just be more messed up." Mary stopped. "But you know that, Hannah. Let's forget the bullshit." She held out her hand. "Will you give me the gun or not?"

Hannah wet her lips. "You know I love you?"

"Yes. I know, you told me."

Hannah wept quietly. "Then you know I can't shoot you."

Mary shook her head. "You fooled me at the barn. Honestly I never know what you're going to do next."

Hannah lowered the gun for a moment. Then she whipped it up and pressed the barrel to her left temple. She was shaking like someone hooked up to an open wire but her finger was tight around the trigger.

"Like you said, I'm screwed," she whispered. "I have to do it."

Mary was sad. "Are you sure?"

Hannah breathed. "Yeah. It's the only way."

Mary sniffed. "Can I kiss you goodbye?"

Hannah brightened. A faint flash. Not enough.

"Would you?" she asked.

Mary smiled. She stepped forward. "Yeah."

Hannah smiled. She actually closed her eyes and leaned forward.

Mary kissed her on the lips.

Then she slowly reached up and pulled the gun down.

Hannah let her. It was enough after all.

Hannah opened her eyes and stared into Mary's.

"It was worth it," she said softly.

Mary was touched. Relieved. "Really?"

Hannah nodded and dropped the gun to the floor.

"I'll talk to the cops, I'll take the blame for everything. I'll talk to my dad, I'll get you into Stanford."

Mary hugged her. "Hannah."

"Wow," Charlie muttered. "What a day."

Riles and Sharp had to agree. What a night.

**Look for
Christopher Pike's**

TALES OF TERROR

Coming Soon

About the Author

CHRISTOPHER PIKE was born in Brooklyn, New York, but grew up in Los Angeles, where he lives to this day. Prior to becoming a writer, he worked in a factory, painted houses, and programmed computers. His hobbies include astronomy, meditating, running, playing with his nieces and nephews, and making sure his books are prominently displayed in local bookstores. He is the author of *Last Act, Spellbound, Gimme a Kiss, Remember Me, Scavenger Hunt, Final Friends* 1, 2, and 3, *Fall into Darkness, See You Later, Witch, Die Softly, Bury Me Deep, Whisper of Death, Chain Letter 2: The Ancient Evil, Master of Murder, Monster, Road to Nowhere, The Eternal Enemy, The Immortal, The Wicked Heart, The Midnight Club, The Last Vampire, The Last Vampire 2: Black Blood, The Last Vampire 3: Red Dice, Remember Me 2: The Return, Remember Me 3: The Last Story, The Lost Mind, The Visitor, The Last Vampire 4: Phantom, The Last Vampire 5: Evil Thirst, the Last Vampire 6: Creatures of Forever, Execution of Innocence, Tales of Terror #1, The Star Group, The Hollow Skull, Tales of Terror #2, Magic Fire,* and *The Grave,* all available from Archway Paperbacks. *Slumber Party, Weekend, Chain Letter,* and *Sati*—an adult novel about a very unusual lady—are also by Mr. Pike.

RICHIE TANKERSLEY
CUSICK